20¢

A
Harlequin
Romance

WELCOME

TO THE WONDERFUL WORLD
OF *Harlequin Romances*

Interesting, informative and entertaining,
each Harlequin Romance portrays an appealing
and original love story. With a varied array
of settings, we may lure you on an African safari,
to a quaint Welsh village, or an exotic riviera
location — anywhere and everywhere that adventurous
men and women fall in love.

As publishers of Harlequin Romances, we're
extremely proud of our books. Since 1949,
Harlequin Enterprises has built its publishing
reputation on the solid base of quality and
originality. Our stories are the most popular
paperback romances sold in North America; every
month, eight new titles are released and sold at
nearly every book-selling store in Canada and the
United States.

A free catalogue listing all available Harlequin Romances
can be yours by writing to the

HARLEQUIN READER SERVICE,
(In the U.S.) M.P.O. Box 707, Niagara Falls, N.Y. 14302
(In Canada) Stratford, Ontario, Canada. N5A 6W4

or use order coupon at back of books.

We sincerely hope you enjoy reading
this Harlequin Romance.

Yours truly,

THE PUBLISHERS
Harlequin Romances

THE SLENDER THREAD

by

YVONNE WHITTAL

Harlequin Books

TORONTO • LONDON • NEW YORK • AMSTERDAM • SYDNEY • WINNIPEG

Original hardcover edition published in 1976
by Mills & Boon Limited

ISBN 0-373-02002-3

Harlequin edition published September 1976

Printed in Canada

CHAPTER ONE

It was summer in the Cape and, despite the sweltering heat, the city's population was swelling with the influx of tourists for the December holidays. As the holiday spirit prevailed and grew to a crescendo, it became increasingly difficult to acquire accommodation at the hotels and camping sites.

Cape Malays, with their shrewd business sense, were luring visitors to their colourful stalls in the market place, enticing money from their pockets with fresh fruit and flowers, and near-primitive mementoes. Shop windows were decorated for the Christmas season, while festive lights had been erected across the Heeren-gracht and down the length of Adderley Street.

The best wines were brought up from the cellars to place before the guests, who dined lavishly and expensively by night, and spent their days languishing in the sun.

From the window of one of the most modern buildings in the centre of the city, an elderly man stood looking out upon the midday traffic, oblivious of the seemingly carefree hustle and bustle in the street below. He had just been informed that his only daughter, Catherine, would have to spend the rest of her life chained to a wheelchair, and the acceptance of this fact was by no means easy.

He turned to face the other occupant in the room. 'Is there absolutely nothing more that can be done for her?' Charles Anderson asked with a look of such infinite sadness on his face that Dr. David Marsden cast his eyes downward to the file before him and unnecessarily rearranged its contents.

'Believe me, Charles,' he replied eventually, 'I've done all in my power to help her. There's nothing more I can do, but—' David Marsden checked himself in time. He had thought of something, but it would be cruel to build up hopes which could quite possibly be dashed to the ground once more.

'Another operation—'

'Would be far too dangerous to even consider,' he interrupted Charles Anderson. 'A nerve in the spinal column has been damaged . . .'

He went on explaining the intricate details of the injury, but Charles was no longer listening. His thoughts were with his daughter, who was at that moment waiting patiently for him to return home with the results of the latest tests and X-rays. She had been confident that at last there would be something they could do for her, and her eagerness for him to take this trip into town had fanned the fire of hope in his own heart. She had assured him that there would be no need for him to be troubled, for she would be well cared for by their coloured servant, Sarah, who had been like a mother to Catherine ever since his wife had died, so many years ago. What was he going to tell her? How was he going to face her with the news David Marsden had imparted to him? The tests; the X-rays; the therapy; the weeks she had spent lying flat on her back. It had all been in vain!

He was jerked back to the present by a hand gently shaking his shoulder.

'Are you all right, Charles?'

He looked up at the young surgeon in bewilderment. 'Yes . . . yes, I think so.' He got to his feet and sighed. 'Well, that's that! All that's left now is for me to break the news to Catherine, and God knows I'm not looking

6

forward to it.'

David Marsden was still a comparatively young man in his early thirties. He loved his job, but it was on occasions such as these that he fervently wished he had chosen a totally different profession. Ruefully he watched Charles Anderson leave his office, his shoulders hunched, his footsteps dragging. As the door closed behind that dejected figure, David cursed himself for his own inadequacy.

Charles drove home disconsolately. It was not far to his home in Constantia, yet the journey appeared to be shorter than usual. Or was it perhaps the unpleasant task of informing Catherine of the final results which made him wish that he lived at the other end of the world?

When he eventually drove through the gates of his home, De Rust, he had a hollow feeling at the pit of his stomach, and he hoped that Catherine had taken his advice and had gone to her room to rest. It would at least grant him a slight respite during which he could prepare himself for the ordeal ahead.

He parked his car under the pergola and stared for a moment at the crimson bougainvillaea ranking profusely along it. How beautiful it looked at this time of the year, he thought as he stepped out on to the driveway and walked along the flagged pathway.

As he reached the terrace, the delicate perfume of the roses wafted up towards him and he turned, admiring their colourful blooms in the brilliant sunshine. He must remember to ask Joseph to remove the dead buds, he thought. He would pick Catherine a bunch of roses first thing in the morning when dew drops were still quivering on their petals.

Joseph had been his gardener for longer than he

could remember, and when Catherine's mother died, it was Joseph who brought his wife, Sarah, to look after Catherine, who was but a small child at the time.

With a sigh Charles opened the oak door with its coloured window panes, and walked hesitantly into the thickly carpeted entrance hall. He was not in the habit of drinking during the day, but a little brandy was just what he needed to calm him, he decided as he entered the living-room. He had barely taken the first sip when a sound behind him made him turn sharply.

Catherine was entering the room in her wheelchair, wheeling it expertly in his direction. Her coppery hair had been cut short since the accident so that it could be cared for without much effort, and it now curled about her face, giving it an elfin quality which was enormously appealing. Her green eyes were set slightly far apart above a tip-tilted nose, and the generous mouth showed signs of the suffering she had endured during the past months.

She was an attractive girl, but it was the expressiveness in her eyes that caught the attention and held one spellbound. She smiled hopefully, displaying even, white teeth, and Charles felt as though his heart was being wrenched from his breast. He gulped down the remainder of his drink and thumped his empty glass on to the tray.

'What's the matter, Daddy?' she asked, the smile fading from her lips as she regarded him steadily.

'Cathy . . .' He groped for the right words, but they evaded him. He wished desperately that somehow he could be relieved of this task he had to perform, but it was a foolish sentiment. There was no one he could turn to in this moment of stress.

Catherine witnessed her father's discomfort with a feeling of despair. She knew him too well not to realize

8

that whatever it was he had to tell her, it would certainly not be what she had hoped for.

'There's nothing more they can do for me, is there?' she asked quietly, knowing, without being told, what lay behind his silent efforts.

Charles nodded and kneeled by her chair. His grey head went down on to her lap and she stroked his hair gently, her touch light and soothing. The future looked suddenly dull and gloomy, with the prospect of having to spend the rest of her life in a wheelchair. She had her books, she thought dispiritedly, for she had always been fond of reading. But even that could not compensate fully for the fact that her limbs were useless.

Charles lifted his head, murmuring apologetically. 'Don't worry, Daddy,' she comforted him bravely, 'it's not the end of the world, you know. Perhaps some time in the future someone might discover something new ... new treatment, or perhaps an operation. Who knows?' The husky quality in her voice was suddenly intensified as their hands met and clung.

In Johannesburg the following morning, Dr. Paul de Meillon was having a late breakfast in his hotel suite while glancing through the newspaper. He had come to South Africa on a lecture tour and was due to fly back to France that evening. It had been an enjoyable trip and he had made a firm decision to return to this country some day in order that he might see more of it. The people had overwhelmed him with their hospitality and he was returning to France with several invitations to pay a return visit to the country he had heard so much about.

Paul de Meillon threw the paper aside, and sat for a moment rubbing his chin thoughtfully, his breakfast forgotten. He would have liked to have been able to contact his old friend David Marsden before returning, but unfortunately he had no idea where to start looking. There had not been time to make extensive enquiries and, regretfully, he resolved to endeavour to trace David on his next visit.

The ringing of the telephone interrupted his thoughts and, dropping his table napkin on to the table, he went to answer it.

'De Meillon,' he said abruptly into the mouthpiece.

'Paul!' a voice exclaimed at the other end. 'I've been telephoning almost every respectable hotel in Johannesburg in an effort to trace you. It's David Marsden speaking. Remember me?'

'David, *mon ami*! How good it is to hear your voice again,' Paul de Meillon greeted heartily. 'I have just this moment been thinking of you. Where are you telephoning from?'

'Paul, you old rascal!' David almost shouted. 'I'm telephoning from Cape Town. Why didn't you contact me?'

'I did not know your address,' Paul informed him.

'Look,' David said quickly, 'are you in a tearing hurry to get back to France?'

'No. I can delay my departure.'

'Good. I've got an interesting case here I would appreciate your opinion on,' David said. 'Right up your alley, my friend. Care to come and have a look?'

'If it means seeing you again, *mon ami*, then I shall come.'

'Wonderful!' David replied excitedly. 'When can I expect you? Today?'

Paul de Meillon laughed good-humouredly. 'As soon as I can get a flight down to Cape Town. Give me your number and I shall telephone you, *mon ami*.'

It was early evening when Dr. Paul de Meillon arrived at D.F. Malan Airport, Cape Town. David Marsden was there to meet him, and after dispensing with the customary formalities, they made their way swiftly to where David had parked his car.

'I'm so glad you could manage to stay a few days longer, Paul,' David remarked as he weaved his way through the traffic. 'Can I make a shrewd guess and say your reason is not so much the interesting case I have lined up for you, but more likely a beautiful blonde, with curves in all the right places?'

Paul threw his head back and laughed heartily. 'Not this time, my friend,' he replied, settling back in his seat. 'You seem to have forgotten that this was a business trip. My pleasure does not come into it at all.'

'Oh, come now, Paul,' David teased, slowing down at a robot. 'Women have always found you irresistible, and you know it.'

'Can I help it when women clamour for my attentions?' Paul retaliated. 'No, *mon ami*, you know I have had very little time to indulge in the affairs of the heart.' He glanced at his friend. 'Why have you not married yet?'

David Marsden shrugged his shoulders. 'Haven't had the time to go looking for the right woman yet.'

It was not long before they arrived at a luxury block of flats and, taking his suitcase off the back seat, Paul followed David inside. On the sixth floor they stepped out of the lift and, taking a bunch of keys from his pocket, David unlocked the door to his flat.

'Come inside and make yourself at home,' he invited, and Paul de Meillon looked about him appreciatively for a moment before doing exactly as his host had suggested.

That evening as they sat under a star-studded sky

drinking coffee on the balcony, Paul asked: 'This case you were talking about on the telephone – is it one of your patients?'

David glanced at him quickly. 'Yes, she's a patient of mine.'

'It is a girl, then?' Paul de Meillon smiled. 'Now I am very interested.'

'I was hoping you would be, Paul,' David admitted seriously. 'That was why I was spending so much time and effort to contact you.'

'You would then not object if I take a look at her X-rays in the morning, and read through your reports?'

'I would be only too pleased if you *would*, Paul,' David replied gratefully. Paul de Meillon was a brilliant neuro-surgeon. He had already made a name for himself by performing the most miraculous operations, and was senior surgeon at a neuro-clinic in France. 'You can make use of my office in the morning while I'm up at the hospital.'

When David Marsden returned to his office just before lunch the following day, he found Paul pacing the floor restlessly. David observed him in silence for a long time, sensing the uneasy air of indecision that surrounded this brilliant man.

Realizing that he was no longer alone, Paul ceased his pacing, and dropped the file he was holding on to the desk.

'Can you get this girl into hospital for a few days? I would like to carry out a few more intensive tests on her before I decide.' He stood regarding David agitatedly with his hands thrust deeply into his trouser pockets. 'Can this be done?'

'It not only *can* be done, it *will* be done!' David replied with determination.

Catherine Anderson considered further tests quite unnecessary, and informed David thus when he approached her later that day. Less than two days ago he had told her father that nothing more could be done for her.

'Why continue with tests which merely exhaust me and serve no other purpose?' she asked obstinately.

'I have a reason for asking this of you, Cathy,' he pleaded, loath to mention Paul's name at that stage. 'Come into hospital tomorrow and let us complete this last series of tests. Will you?'

She considered this for a moment in silence. Hope fluttered like a frightened little bird in her breast, but she crushed it instantly for fear of further disappointment.

'Will this really be for the last time?' she asked quietly. 'Will I be left in peace after these tests to adjust myself to this new way of life?'

David regarded her seriously. If this girl were to give him the slightest encouragement, whether she were an invalid or not, he would propose to her instantly, he thought. He surfaced from his thoughts suddenly to find her looking at him curiously.

'Well?' she asked, waiting.

'Yes, Cathy, this will be the last time,' he promised.

Charles Anderson drove his daughter to the hospital the following morning with a certain amount of trepidation, and remained just long enough to see her settled before leaving for his office.

On her own, Catherine settled back against the pillows and wondered dejectedly how long she would have to remain in hospital on this occasion. Her father had not been too thrilled at the idea, and had voiced his opinion loudly. 'It's like trying to skin a cat twice,' he had said, and she was inclined to agree with him. Sighing heavily, she flicked idly through the pages of a magazine.

When Paul de Meillon entered the private ward with David, something stirred within him at the sight of the lovely girl lying sleeping on the high hospital bed with its snowy white linen. His glance swept from the dark lashes fanning her pale cheeks to the small slender hands lying above the covers. He felt almost as though he were trespassing as his glance swept upwards once more to her closed eyelids. He was intensely curious to discover the colour of her eyes, and almost willed her to awaken.

'Lovely, isn't she?' David asked softly beside him, and Paul was aware of something more than admiration in his friend's eyes as he looked down upon the sleeping girl.

Catherine stirred then and opened her eyes to find David Marsden standing beside her bed. But he was not alone. Beside him stood the most attractive man she had ever seen, and he was gazing at her intently – so intently, in fact, that she felt herself blushing profusely. He had about him an air of confidence that was somehow reassuring, and she wondered confusedly who he was. Tall, with broad shoulders tapering down to slim hips, he looked more like a film star and quite out of place in a hospital ward.

'I would like you to meet a friend of mine,' David was saying. 'Dr. Paul de Meillon. He came out from France on a short lecture tour and has decided to stay a while longer. Paul, this is Catherine Anderson whom I've told you so much about.'

The Frenchman stepped forward then, took her hand in his and carried it to his lips while his dark eyes held hers captive. 'I am honoured to meet you, *mademoiselle.'*

'How do you do,' she managed breathlessly. He spoke with an accent that was both pleasing and unusual.

'I hope you do not mind being ordered back here so soon after the last time?' he asked, releasing her hand.

Catherine could have replied that she did not mind at all, not after meeting him, but she merely smiled. 'David – Dr. Marsden was quite insistent, so you see I had very little choice.'

'I can almost promise you, Mademoiselle Anderson, your stay will not be a lengthy one.'

'Dr. de Meillon is a neuro-surgeon, Cathy,' David enlightened her. 'He's very interested in the extent of your injuries.'

'Why?'

The two men glanced quickly at each other at the directness of her question, and Catherine sensed instantly that something was being withheld from her. It frightened her. David Marsden noticed this and pressed her hand reassuringly before turning to Paul.

'Perhaps it will be better to tell her the truth.'

Paul de Meillon nodded understandingly. 'Perhaps you are right, *mon ami*. Why don't you go and visit that patient of yours while I explain to Mademoiselle Anderson? I shall meet you at the front entrance later.'

'Very well.' David turned and winked at Catherine. 'If you need any help, just scream. The Sister's office is just across the passage.'

'You will have Mademoiselle Anderson thinking that I am a monster,' Paul smiled, taking David's teasing remark in his stride.

'Just remember what I said, Catherine,' David continued laughingly.

'I'll remember,' she promised lightly.

Left alone with Dr. Paul de Meillon, she was aware of his dark eyes appraising her once more, and a tremor ran through her. Fear? Certainly not, she told herself, but it certainly was a sensation she had not experienced before. She had never yet found it difficult to behave naturally in a man's company, but Paul de Meillon unnerved her, for some unknown reason. David had laughingly remarked that she need only scream and the Sister would come running. Would that be necessary? she wondered crazily.

'You shall not have to scream for help, *mademoiselle*,' he reassured her as though he had been able to read her thoughts. 'I am really quite harmless.'

Catherine blushed becomingly and avoided the gentle mockery in his eyes. 'I'm not afraid of you, Dr. de Meillon, only of what you have to tell me.'

'What I have to tell you need cause you no alarm,' he told her smilingly as he pulled a chair closer to the bed and sat down.

She glanced at him surreptitiously. His crisp dark hair was brushed back severely, as though it had a tendency to fall across his broad forehead. His finely chiselled mouth, with the slightly full, sensuous lower lip, had a look of sternness about it which left her in no doubt that where it concerned his work, he was a perfectionist almost to the point of cruelty. And this was confirmed by the determination in his square chin. He was, however, smiling at her now and Catherine relaxed.

'You have been observing me, *mademoiselle*,' he said with that slight hint of mockery in his voice. 'May I ask what you have decided?'

A redness seeped into her cheeks once more, but she

replied without hesitation. 'I think you can be ruthless when you want your instructions carried out, but I agree that there is no cause for alarm.'

'*Merci*, Mademoiselle Anderson. Now,' his face sobered, 'it is time for a serious talk. During the past two years great strides have been made in the field of neurosurgery. New methods of surgery have been developed. Although some have been successful, others are only in the experimental stages.'

'Are you telling me that you can do something for me?' Catherine asked hopefully.

'No.'

'Oh.' Her frail hopes plummeted to the earth like a bird shot in flight. 'I thought . . . when you . . . that you . . .' She faltered, catching her trembling lower lip between her teeth.

Paul de Meillon sat forward in his chair. 'I cannot tell you what you wish to hear unless further tests are carried out. That is why you are here, and that is why I am going to ask you not to build castles which may come tumbling down. Be patient and time will tell.'

Catherine returned home after a few days to begin the agonizing period of waiting. Common sense forced her to quell even the slightest hope, but it was a near impossible task. It was Christmas Eve, and as yet she had heard nothing from David or Dr. de Meillon. What had they decided? How much longer would she still have to wait? Her father, too, was beginning to feel the strain, but he at least had his work to fill his days.

Sitting in her wheelchair in front of her bedroom window, she could see the Christmas tree lights flicking on and off in the living-room window of the

17

house across the street. What fun it had always been to decorate the tree for Christmas! This year they had not bothered. She would not even have bought her father a present had Sarah not pointed out the fact one afternoon.

'Miss Cathy,' she had said, 'you can't let Christmas go by without giving your father a present. *Ag, nee*! It will be too bad!'

Catherine admitted shamefacedly that this was true. 'But how can I go into town when I'm tied to this chair?'

'I'll tell you what, Miss Cathy,' Sarah had suggested after a moment's consideration. 'I will go and buy your father something. You just tell me what he would like.'

The very next afternoon she had gone to town and brought home the small portable tape recorder which her father had been threatening to buy so often. Excitedly they had wrapped the present and hid it carefully at the bottom of Catherine's wardrobe.

She sighed heavily. This was a time of rejoicing, yet it felt as though a piece of lead had lodged where her heart should be.

Twin beams of light turned unexpectedly into their driveway, and Catherine wheeled herself closer to the window in an effort to discover who the unexpected visitor could be. To her surprise she saw Dr. Paul de Meillon step from the car and make his way up the flagged path to the front door. Quickly she wheeled herself from her room. Did he have news? she wondered, suppressing the shiver of hope that surged through her.

The front door bell rang as Catherine left her room and, remaining hidden in the shadows, she watched her father stride to the door and open it.

'Dr de Meillon!' he exclaimed. 'What a pleasant surprise!'

'I do hope I have not come at an inopportune moment?' she heard Paul de Meillon say apologetically as he stepped into the hall, his foreign good looks increased by the gentleness of the old-fashioned chandelier that hung from the ceiling.

'My dear fellow,' Charles Anderson assured him, 'you couldn't be more welcome.'

The two men stood talking for a moment, while Catherine was acutely conscious of the heavy beating of her heart. What a magnificent-looking man he was, she thought. He gestured expressively as she spoke, and even at a distance one had to admire the supple strength of his well-shaped hands.

He obviously sensed that he was being observed, for he turned suddenly to look searchingly into the shadows. He surely must be able to see her, so there was no sense in remaining hidden much longer, Catherine decided as she wheeled herself forward.

'Good evening, Dr. de Meillon,' she greeted as she came closer.

'*Bonsoir, mademoiselle*,' he answered, taking her hand and bending over it. His lips brushed her fingers and once again, as on the first occasion she had met him, a tingling sensation quivered up the length of her arm. 'You are well?' he asked, holding her hand captive in his for longer than was necessary.

'Yes,' she replied nervously, 'quite well, thank you.'

'*Bòn*! I have some news for you and your father.'

'Then let's go through to the living-room,' Charles suggested, pushing Catherine's chair and leading the way. 'We may as well talk in comfort. Would you like a glass of wine, Dr. de Meillon, or would you prefer a brandy?' he offered after they were seated.

'I think I would like some wine, *monsieur*,' Paul replied, making himself comfortable in an easy chair and stretching his long legs before him. 'I am no connoisseur, but your Cape wine is delectable to the palate.'

'Ah, yes, I have some wine here from a Franschhoek winery,' Charles said, pouring the crimson liquid into wine goblets. 'It's one of the best.' He handed their guest his drink. 'Try it.'

Paul de Meillon took a mouthful and rolled it appreciatively about his tongue before swallowing it. '*Magnifique*!' he exclaimed with delight. 'I have never yet tasted anything so good.'

Satisfied, Charles handed a glass of wine to Catherine, and took one for himself. 'Merry Christmas, Dr. de Meillon,' he said, raising his glass.

'*Oui, monsieur* and *mademoiselle*, Merry Christmas.'

They drained their glasses and chatted amicably for a while until, quite suddenly, an apprehensive silence prevailed. It was as though they had all been putting off the inevitable, but found they could no longer continue to do so. Finally it was Catherine who broached the subject which reigned supreme in their minds. She had sensed her father's anxiety and Dr. de Meillon's withdrawal, and knew that it was futile to delay matters further. Steeling herself for whatever was to follow, she asked:

'What were the results of the tests, Dr. de Meillon?'

Charles Anderson sucked his breath in sharply through clenched teeth, while Paul de Meillon's dark eyes looked steadily into Catherine's.

'*Mademoiselle*,' he began cautiously, 'what I am going to tell, both yourself and your father, will need careful consideration. I do not want you to answer me too hastily. You must think about it for a time.' He paused a moment as if to make sure that he had their full attention. 'There is an operation I can perform, but . . . and I must stress this fact . . . the chances that you will walk again are fifty-fifty. If this operation is not successful, it may spoil your chances of any further surgery. It is a risk.'

'And if the operation is successful?' Catherine asked with a calmness that belied the tumult within her.

'Then, *mademoiselle*,' he made an eloquent gesture with his hands, 'you shall surely walk again.'

There was a short silence while they digested this information. Charles Anderson offered Paul a cigarette and took one for himself, but his hands shook to such an extent that Paul had to remove the lighter from his fingers to light their cigarettes with his own steady hand.

Charles blew the smoke forcibly towards the ceiling. 'I don't know what to say.'

'I do,' Catherine said quietly but firmly. 'If you're willing to perform the operation, Dr. de Meillon, then I'm more than willing to take the risk.'

CHAPTER TWO

THE drone of hospital activity soothed Catherine as she lay in her bed watching a dove that had settled on the ledge outside her window. The Christmas and New Year festivities were over and businesses were reverting back to normal procedures. Holidaymakers were drifting inland to their homes, their season of lazy inactivity something they would discuss enthusiastically for several months.

The dove on the window ledge had satisfied its curiosity and, deciding that nothing of interest lay beyond those glass window panes, it flew away quickly. Catherine sighed ecstatically. How delightful to be free from bondage; free to go where it pleased as she had been freed just a few weeks ago. Dr. Paul de Meillon had, with his clever brain and supple hands, performed yet another miraculous operation.

Catherine could not help smiling as she recalled the evening Paul de Meillon had paid them a visit to confront them with the news that there was, after all, an operation he could perform which might allow her to walk again. Without a moment's hesitation she had jumped at the chance, and despite his insistence that she should give the matter some thought, Catherine could not be dissuaded. Less than a week later she was wheeled into the operating theatre.

'There is still time to change your mind,' Paul de Meillon had informed her moments before the anaesthetist plunged the needle into her arm.

'I've prayed about this,' she had replied with an inner conviction. 'This was meant to be.'

His eyes had looked down at her intently over the top of his mask. 'I will do my best.'

'I know you will,' she had replied, and Paul de Meillon then nodded to the anaesthetist that he was ready.

That was almost a month ago. The operation had been a complete success and with careful treatment, Dr. de Meillon had stated, there was no reason why she should not walk again. In the interim he had returned to France with the promise to return as soon as he could. He had every intention of following her recovery through to the end, he had told her.

David Marsden had taken over again in his friend's absence, and carried out his instructions with meticulous care. Catherine had laughed at him one morning after he had severely reprimanded the Sister for neglecting to give her a massage.

'I wouldn't like Paul to return and find we've slipped up on any part of his prescribed treatment,' he had explained agitatedly.

Yes, Catherine had thought, Paul de Meillon would not tolerate even the slightest misdemeanour. She had been right about him. Where was he now? she wondered as she brought her thoughts back to the present and tried to sleep. Would he really come back as he had promised, or would his commitments keep him there in France? After all, David Marsden could cope very well without him, and there was actually no real need for him to return. But he *was* needed. *She* needed him!

Moving about restlessly in her bed, she tried, unsuccessfully, not to think of him. She had caught him studying her intently on numerous occasions, but each time she returned his glance, his eyes had become veiled, his look guarded. What had he been thinking on those occasions? she wondered. What was it about the man that interested her so?

Tiredness finally swept all thoughts from her mind and she slept fitfully until the evening meal was brought to her.

'Are you expecting visitors this evening, Miss Anderson?' the young nurse asked when she returned later to remove the tray, and tidy up the bed.

'Not tonight,' Catherine replied smilingly. 'My father has gone on a short business trip to Johannesburg for a few days, and there's no one else.'

'Not even a boy-friend.'

'No.'

'Shame,' the nurse clucked sympathetically while fixing Catherine's pillows. 'If you get lonely just ring the bell, and I'll come and talk to you for a while.'

'Won't you be busy tonight?' Catherine asked, settling back comfortably against the pillows.

'The nights are normally very quiet,' she told Catherine. 'Sometimes there's nothing to do, but at other times ...' She rolled her eyes towards the ceiling. 'Phew!'

'Let's hope that tonight is a quiet night for you,' Catherine said politely as the young nurse prepared to leave.

'I hope so too, Miss Anderson,' the nurse said as she disappeared into the corridor.

Catherine picked up a book and started reading. Fortunately she had a private ward, so that when the visitors started filtering in they hardly ever disturbed her.

'Someone to see you, Miss Anderson,' the same young nurse announced a short while later, and Catherine looked up in surprise to see a young man coming towards her.

'Ronnie!' she exclaimed indignantly. 'What are you

doing here?'

'What a way to greet an old friend, sweetie,' he said, bending over to kiss her. Catherine turned her face away, and the kiss landed somewhere on her cheek.

She had not dreamed that she would ever see Ronald Jansen again. Not after what had happened. His clothes were just as flashy as ever, she thought, as he pulled a chair closer to sit down. His blond hair was combed and cut in the latest style, and but for the scar above his left eye, he looked just the same. His face was weak and without character, and she was amazed to think that she had once been foolish enough to think that she was in love with him. Oh, yes, on the surface he appeared to all girls like a young Apollo, but underneath he was a spineless creature with no thought for anyone but himself. He had proved that irrevocably.

'Why are you looking at me like that, sweetie?' he asked sorrowfully. 'Aren't you glad I came to see you?'

'Frankly, Ronnie, no! I'd thought that after what had happened I would never see you again. In fact, I'd fervently hoped so.'

'You're not still angry with me because of the accident, are you?'

Angry? Would one entertain such an emotion as anger when one had been robbed of the use of one's legs? No! How little Ronnie cared or understood. How infantile his reasoning compared to that of a man like Paul de Meillon.

'You'd drunk too much that night at the party,' she accused him, her eyes mirroring her disgust.

'Now, Cathy, let's not go over all that again.'

'I begged you to let me drive the car,' she continued as if he had not spoken. 'Instead you lost your temper, and to prove your sobriety you deliberately drove faster than was necessary. I'm not surprised you lost control of the car, considering you could hardly control your legs for the purpose of walking.'

'You're exaggerating, sweetie,' he denied with an air of defiance.

'Am I, Ronnie?' she asked sarcastically, recalling vividly the incidents which occurred on that frightful night. 'If I hadn't held your arm as we left the house you would have fallen down the steps on to the driveway. Do you call that exaggeration?'

'Don't you appreciate the fact that I walked nearly two miles that night to get help for you?' he asked sullenly.

'Oh, yes, I do appreciate it. But you didn't bother returning to make sure that I actually got that help,' she replied scathingly. 'When the police arrived at your home a short while later you were in bed, fast asleep.'

'You must understand, sweetie,' he defended himself, 'when I arrived home that night, I was in such a state of shock that my mother immediately called the doctor in to stitch the cut above my eye, and she insisted afterwards that I should go straight to bed.'

'That's no excuse for letting six months go by without inquiring after the health of someone you professed to love,' she reminded him unemotionally.

Ronald Jansen shifted uncomfortably. He was agitated, she could tell. Things were not working out the way he had planned, and if he thought that they could just pick up where they had left off, he was very much mistaken. Six months ago she might have been just as shallow as he was, but after the injury she had suffered, she had realized that there was more to life than merely flitting from one gay party to the next. She had changed, she knew, but whereas she had grown up suddenly, Ronnie had remained the callous youth he was.

'I'm sorry I never came to see you, Cathy,' he apologized. 'I've been busy.'

'Yes, I'm sure you've been busy,' she agreed sarcastically. 'Busy dividing your time between a dozen or so girls.'

Ronnie at least had the grace to blush. 'That's not fair, Cathy.'

'Have you been fair to me?' she asked angrily, wishing he would go and leave her alone. She was becoming physically and mentally exhausted by this senseless discussion.

'Sweetie, let's stop this bickering,' he begged, regaining his composure and taking a firm grip on her arms. 'You love me, you know you do.'

'Why, you conceited . . .' A suitable word to express her loathing evaded her. 'Will you get out of here and don't bother ever to return!'

Ronnie merely laughed, sliding his arms about her and pressing her close to him. 'Don't try to deny it, sweetie,' he laughed, bringing his lips closer to hers. 'You're crazy about me – always have been.'

He had certainly regained his earlier egotism rather suddenly and, as in the days when he had been her steady boy-friend, he was trying to overpower her with kisses.

'Go away! Leave me alone!' she cried, her inability to fight him off filling her with desperation. 'I suppose your girl-friends have all seen through you,' she voiced her suspicion. 'When you heard I would soon be walking again, you were conceited enough to think I would be only too willing and eager to take you back. Well, you're mistaken!'

'Kiss me, sweetie,' he insisted confidently, 'and afterwards you can tell me if I'm not right.'

Cathy twisted her head from side to side in an effort to avoid his lips, but to no avail. His mouth closed over hers in a hot, passionate kiss, which was intended to make her surrender, but only served to nauseate her.

'Tell me now that you don't love me,' he demanded triumphantly with his lips close to her ear.

'I hate you!' she cried. 'If you don't leave my room immediately, I'm going to ring this bell and call the Sister!'

'Oh, no, you won't, my sweet,' he laughed, imprisoning her hand. 'Give us another kiss.'

'No!'

The room started spinning about her, and Ronnie's face became contorted as it retreated into the distance. Oh, God, she thought, I'm going to faint. Struggling up through the enveloping darkness, she heard a familiar voice say: 'I think, *monsieur*, you have upset my patient quite enough for one evening.'

'Paul!' she sobbed before sinking into the bottomless pit of oblivion.

A heavy hand gripped Ronnie's shoulder and he was unceremoniously jerked to his feet. As he confronted Paul de Meillon's large frame, his eyes widened, but he lost nothing of his bravado. 'Who are you? What do you want? What right have you to interfere?'

Paul de Meillon's face hardened as a cold anger beseiged him. 'As Mademoiselle Anderson's doctor I have every right to do so. You are hampering my patient's recovery, and while she is in my care I will not have you visiting her again. Do I make myself clear?'

Ronnie looked up at him defiantly for a moment, but when he saw the violence on the Frenchman's face, he lost his haughtiness and beat a hasty retreat.

Paul sat down hastily in the chair vacated by the

young man and gently chafed her wrists. Who was the young fool, he wondered, who had had the temerity to force his attentions on this girl? Her lover, perhaps? No, he rejected the idea; it had been quite apparent that she had had no desire to be mauled by the young cad.

Her eyelids flickered and then flew open. 'Ronnie?' she asked fearfully.

'Do not be afraid,' Paul informed her quietly, as he released her hands. 'Your friend has left – I saw to that.'

'He's not my friend, Dr. de Meillon.'

'You called me Paul a moment ago,' he observed dryly.

Catherine blushed furiously. So she had not imagined it, then. 'Forgive me, Dr. de Meillon – I really don't know what you must think of me.'

'Please!' he held up his hand to silence her. 'I would prefer it if you called me so. We shall be spending much time together in the future. There will be occasions when you will hate me for the things I will make you do, so it is better that we start off as friends. Not so, Catherine?'

'Do you always allow your patients to call you by your first name, Dr. de Mei – Paul?' An amused smile hovered about his lips as she stumbled over his name.

'Only those who have hair that looks as though the sun has settled in it.' He twisted a curl about his forefinger and Catherine's treacherous pulse quickened. 'There is also another stipulation. They must have green eyes with flecks of gold in their depths.' His fingers trailed across her flushed cheek. 'So you see, Catherine, you qualify on both counts.'

Was he just teasing, or was he actually flirting with her? she wondered frantically. He exuded a magnetism that drew her to him like a moth to a flame, and she was surprised to find that she was not exactly putting up much of a struggle. It frightened her, this awareness of a man whom she had seen only a few times. It was a known fact that many women thought themselves in love with their doctors because they mistook gratitude for love. The slender thread between the two emotions was almost indefinable, but it was there all the same.

'You are thoughtful, *chérie*. What are you thinking?'

'I was thinking, Dr. de – Paul,' again the amused smile touched his lips, 'that you must be teasing me, and that's not very kind of you.'

He considered this for a moment. What would she say, he wondered gravely, if he should tell her that no other woman had ever succeeded in captivating him as she had done from the moment he had seen her lying so helpless in the hospital? That his anger against the young man whom he had found molesting her had been fired by jealousy.

'Perhaps you are right, *chérie*,' he agreed, shrugging his broad shoulders. 'It was not very kind of me to tease you, but I am very serious when I say it must be Paul from now on. Yes?'

'Yes,' she smiled up at him shyly.

'Yes, who?' he teased again.

'Yes, Paul.' His light summer suit was superbly cut and clung to him as though his tailor had found great pleasure in accentuating his athletic build. His physique matched his character, of this she was sure. Paul de Meillon was the kind of man who would be master in his own home at all times; who would not tolerate insubordination from his wife. She had never enquired whether he was married or not, and the thought suddenly alarmed her. She had to know. 'Did your wife not object to you coming all the way to South Africa again?'

'I have no wife, *chérie*,' he smiled. 'Just a sister who is still at school in England.'

'Oh!' Relief clamoured through her veins. He was free! her foolish heart rejoiced. 'Your parents? Are they still living?'

'My mother died soon after Adèle was born. My father never recovered from the loss, and died a few years later.'

'I'm sorry.'

'No matter,' he said abruptly, and changed the subject. 'This young man . . . Ronnie, I think his name is. He is a special friend of yours?'

'He was once.' Catherine told him then of what had transpired moments before he had entered her ward, and how the accident had occurred which had so very nearly robbed her permanently of the use of her legs. Something of the loathing she felt was clearly visible in her eyes as she looked steadily up at him.

'I am sorry now that I did not thrash him,' Paul remarked when she had finished. 'The young fool could have killed you!' he concluded savagely. 'So many young people have lost their lives through carelessness. They drink too much; they drive too fast, and *dieu!* . . . the end is always tragic.'

When he became agitated his accent was more pronounced, she noticed, although at other times his English was perfect. Had he also, like his sister, spent some time in England? Perhaps she would ask him one day, she decided.

'You are growing tired, *petite*,' he remarked, getting to his feet. 'Will you be able to sleep, or must I ask the Sister to give you a sedative?'

'I'll sleep, Paul. Thank you.' She held out her hand and he took it between his own. 'And thank you for coming back.'

31

'Did you think I would not?' he asked in surprise.

'I wasn't sure.'

'I never break a promise, Catherine.' He raised her hand to his lips. 'Now, go to sleep. As from tomorrow you are going to have very little time to rest. I shall give you no peace until the day you can walk. Remember this.'

Paul had meant every word when he had said that she would have little time to rest during the days to come. He had mapped out rigorous daily exercises which he forced her to do quite relentlessly. He bullied and cajoled her until she was ready to drop from sheer fatigue. Her reward was the tingling sensation which increased daily as the life returned to her useless legs, and although she was exhausted at the end of each day, she slept soundly at night to awake refreshed in the morning.

When Paul ordered her to walk between the bars for the first time, she had stared at him in horror.

'I can't!' she exclaimed as her nerves contracted into a tight ball at the pit of her stomach. 'You can't make me do it!'

'*Mon dieu!*' he exploded. 'Have I been wasting my time? If that is so, then I wash my hands of you!' He gestured as though he was literally doing just that, then turned on his heel and strode away angrily.

'Paul! Please come back!'

He halted in his stride and turned to face her, his expression thunderous. The tears sprang to her eyes. 'I'm sorry. I'll do whatever you say.'

At the end of that particular session, Paul picked her up in his arms and, regardless of the physiotherapists and nurses present, he carried her back to her chair as if she were a child.

'Was that so very bad?' he asked, removing his handkerchief from his breast pocket to wipe the perspiration from her brow. 'Was it, *chérie?*' He placed a finger beneath her chin and tilted her face upwards.

When he looked at her in that special way, and spoke with such tenderness, Catherine felt sure that she would be able to climb Table Mountain unaided if he so wished it.

'No,' she admitted. 'It wasn't all that difficult after all.'

When Catherine was finally allowed to return home, she was still walking with the aid of a stick, but this did not alter Charles Anderson's delight at seeing his daughter on her feet once more. He wept for joy when he collected her at the hospital that morning, clasping her to him as though he never wanted to release her again. 'God has been good to us,' he said simply, and Catherine echoed his sentiment.

At De Rust Sarah had literally laid out the red carpet. A meal that more likely resembled a feast was being prepared for Catherine's homecoming, but in the interim tea and home-made biscuits were being served to them on the terrace.

'It's good to have you back with us, Miss Cathy,' she beamed. 'I was just telling Joseph the other night that the house has been too quiet with the master at work all day and with you in hospital. But you're looking so well, Miss Cathy. I can't believe it.'

Sarah stood with her hands clasped together against her ample bosom, her grey hair knotted in the nape of her neck. How familiar and how dear she was, Catherine thought, smiling at her fondly. 'It's good to be back, Sarah, and I hope you won't be bullying me the way Paul has been doing these past few weeks!'

'If you look as well as you do after being bullied, as

you call it,' Charles interrupted laughingly, 'then perhaps we should continue doing just that here at home.'

'*Ja*, the master is right,' Sarah nodded, a twinkle in her eyes. 'You've got rosy cheeks again and don't look as pale as you did.' She took in Catherine's slender figure relaxing in the cane chair. 'You're just a bit thin, Miss Cathy, but we'll soon have you back to what you used to be before the accident.'

'Heaven forbid!' Catherine protested. 'I was overweight and you know it, Sarah, so don't start fattening me up again, or I shall have to go on a starvation diet every alternate week.'

Sarah shook her head as she returned to the kitchen. 'These young people of today, they're always wanting to be thin; always dieting,' she mumbled to herself. 'It's so unhealthy,' she decided, taking a look at the roast in the oven.

A sleek crimson sports car arrived at De Rust the following day with Paul at the wheel, and Catherine was on the terrace to meet him. Dressed in a cream linen suit he looked tanned and extremely virile, and Catherine wondered secretly what he would say if he discovered what a devastating effect he had on her pulse rate. He came up the steps towards her and looked at her critically.

'You are looking well, Catherine,' he remarked as he stood before her. 'You are happy to be home?'

'Yes, thank you, Paul.' A smile hovered about her lips. 'I've been treated royally these last forty-eight hours, and I haven't been bullied once.'

'Then something will have to be done to remedy that,' he announced goodhumouredly as he seated himself opposite her.

'Would you like some tea, Paul?' she asked quickly.

'To tell the truth, *petite*, I have come to ask you to have tea with me,' he announced. 'Do you know of a place we can drive to where there is little noise and a tea room that serves cream scones?'

Catherine laughed mischievously. 'Do you have a sweet tooth, Paul?'

'I must admit that I do,' he replied, grimacing. 'Do you know of such a place, Catherine? And will you come with me?'

'I do, and I would love to come with you,' she agreed, excitement welling up in her. She would be alone with Paul for the first time, and not as in the hospital where there were always nurses and physiotherapists hovering about. 'I'd better tell Sarah, though, otherwise she might worry.'

'Stay where you are,' he ordered. 'I will go and find her.'

He entered the house and returned seconds later to say that all was in order. To her surprise he stooped down and picked her up in his arms. What was he up to now? she wondered nervously as he carried her down the steps and set her down on her feet beside a stone wall.

'Hold on to that for support,' he ordered, and then walked a few paces away. 'Now,' he said, turning, 'come to me.'

Catherine stood petrified. 'You must be mad to think I can walk without the aid of a walking stick!'

'You are going to walk without it today,' he replied quite calmly.

'I can't!' she sobbed.

'Come,' he insisted, spreading his arms wide. 'I shall not let you fall, or hurt yourself.'

Keeping her eyes on him, she found herself obeying. She released her grip on the wall and took the first hesitant step towards him, then another, and yet another, until she fell breathlessly into his arms. 'I walked. I walked without the stick!' she cried, clutching at him.

'But of course you did, *chérie*,' he spoke soothingly somewhere above her head. 'Did you think I would let you do something impossible?'

'No,' she shook her head. 'I just didn't think I could.'

'All you needed was confidence,' he told her. 'Now you are going to hold on to my arm and walk the rest of the way to the car.'

'My stick,' she protested as he hooked her arm through his.

'Not today, *petite*,' he said firmly. 'Today you are going out with me and you are leaving that walking stick behind.'

Catherine obeyed meekly, clutching his arm for support as they walked to where he had parked the car.

'You have not yet told me where we are going,' Paul reminded her after she had directed him a few blocks. He drove superbly for a stranger in Cape Town, she marvelled as she turned to look at him.

'I hope you like flowers, Paul,' she said hesitantly, 'because I'm directing you to the Kirstenbosch Botanical Gardens. It's peaceful there and the tea room serves the most delicious cream scones,' she added impishly.

'*Oui*, the cream scones,' he said, a smile curving about his lips. 'I am looking forward to this visit to your botanical gardens. In the few weeks I have been here I have seen very little of your tourist attractions. This is something I hope to rectify during my last three days in

South Africa.'

A heavy silence descended in the car after that last remark, and Catherine felt as though a hand had reached out and squeezed her heart until it hurt. He was leaving within three days! Just a few miserable days and then she would never see him again. He would return to France, to his clinic, and she would be forgotten while he would remain a part of her for ever, as though indelibly printed on her heart and mind.

'You are very quiet, Catherine,' he remarked eventually, unaware of the effect his lightly spoken words had had on her. 'Are you not feeling well?'

'I – I didn't realize you would be leaving so soon.'

He glanced at her quickly. 'I have been away from the Clinic a long time. They will think I have no intention of returning.'

'I'm sorry,' she apologized shakily. 'It's my fault really that you stayed so long.'

'Do not apologize, Catherine,' he said roughly. 'I chose to remain of my own accord. Your case interested me and that was that, as they say.'

Was that all she was to him? Just a case that interested him? Another achievement up the ladder of success? What an absolute idiot she had been to allow herself to fall in love with him, she admonished herself angrily. The day had somehow been spoilt for her by the knowledge of his imminent departure.

Kirstenbosch was situated against the slopes of Table Mountain. Acres of picturesque gardens where South Africa's indigenous flora were cultivated for all to admire and enjoy. Visitors had a choice of paths which wound their way in amongst the flowers. It was a hot day with not a cloud in sight, even the birds sought the shade and bathed themselves noisily in a small pool amongst the trees.

Seated on a bench nearby, Catherine and Paul watched their antics with amusement.

'There is nothing small about your country,' Paul remarked, lighting a cigarette. 'Everywhere I go there is so much space. Take these gardens, for instance, and the variety of flowers!' He gestured about him. 'I am glad that you have brought me here.'

'This is not quite the right time of the year for Kirstenbosch,' Catherine told him, flicking a beetle from her skirt. 'During October the gardens are always at their best.'

'This pool,' he pointed to where the birds were enjoying their boisterous bath. 'It is an unusual shape and laid out with stones to resemble a bath.'

'That's just what it is,' she laughed. 'It's said that Lady Anne Barnard, during the time when her husband was Colonial Secretary to the Governor, used to slip away from the Castle to come and bathe here.'

'*Mon dieu*! When was this?'

'Somewhere in the 1790s, I think,' she laughed up at him. 'Cape Town has a fascinating history which never tires one hearing about it.'

Paul smoked in silence for a while and then crushed his cigarette underfoot. 'Are you rested, *chérie*? Can we go in search of those cream scones now?'

'Yes, we can,' she agreed laughingly, placing a hand on his arm as they strolled slowly down to the tea room.

Seated eventually at a window with a view of Kirstenbosch against the back drop of Table Mountain, Paul ordered tea and scones, and as they waited he complimented her on her achievement that morning.

'You have done well, Catherine,' he said seriously. 'From now on, no more walking stick. You understand?'

'I understand,' she nodded, and frowned slightly as a thought crossed her mind. 'Paul . . . I shall never be able to thank you enough for what you did for me, and when your account arrives it will be paid instantly, and gladly.'

Paul gestured vaguely. 'There will be no account, Catherine.'

'But—'

'To me, this was an experience I would not have missed. It was a challenge.' He smiled gently. 'You have forgotten, *petite*, I came to you. You did not come to me.'

'Yes, but surely—'

'As payment,' he interrupted, 'you can show me something of your country before I leave. You will do this?'

'You are asking very little of me in return for your services.' She looked at him earnestly. 'It will be a pleasure to show you something of my country, although Cape Town and the surrounding areas are only a small part of it.'

A tremor of excitement quivered through her slender form. They would at least be spending his last few days in South Africa together. It was little consolation to her that it would have to last a lifetime.

The drive to Constantia seemed to pass much too swiftly and soon, too soon, they arrived at De Rust.

'I shall call for you tomorrow morning at nine,' Paul said as he took his leave of her at the front door. 'I leave the planning of this excursion entirely to you.'

Catherine walked slowly to her room after Paul had left. It had been a lovely morning, and for the next three days he would be entirely at her disposal. She had to make them memorable, she decided firmly. Memorable, not only for him, but for herself.

CHAPTER THREE

THE familiar feeling of exhilaration swept through Catherine when the ground dropped away beneath them as the cable car swung its way smoothly up towards the summit of Table Mountain. On a clear day such as this the visibility stretched far beyond the boundaries of the city.

On reaching the summit Paul took her arm as they stepped from the cable car and guided her along the uneven path as they followed the other tourists to a vantage point from where they could admire the view. She shivered involuntarily as the cool breeze whipped across her face.

'You are cold, *chérie?*' Paul asked with concern, placing his arm about her shoulders.

'The sudden drop in temperature caught me a little unaware,' she explained.

The protective warmth of his body so close to hers had an odd effect on her nervous system. Her heart performed odd little jerking movements and she had to suppress the ridiculous desire to turn and bury her face against the broadness of his chest.

'How high are we, Catherine?' he asked as they joined the tourists who stood looking down upon Cape Town, picking out familiar landmarks.

'We're about a thousand metres above sea level, I think.'

Paul whistled softly through his teeth and then, standing behind her, he pointed over her shoulder. 'There are many trees in the centre of the city. Is it a park?'

Intensely aware of his nearness, she followed the line of his arm. 'It's the Municipal Botanic Gardens. They have a wide variety of trees, orchids and ferns, also a scented garden for the blind.'

His breath fanned her cheek and she closed her eyes against the overwhelming desire to lean back against him.

'I'll take you there in a little while,' she promised, moving slightly away from him.

Paul bought picture postcards in the tea room before they left. The tea room was built entirely of rough stones, which was in itself quite picturesque. The descent was equally pleasant, except that Catherine was slightly unnerved by a child who screamed hysterically while pummelling his exasperated mother's chest.

They drove quickly to the gardens and before long they were feeding the pigeons who made a practice of scrounging titbits from the visitors.

'Looking up at the mountain from down here, one would never believe that there are big boulders up there, which does not make the mountain resemble a table at all,' Paul remarked, brushing crumbs from his immaculately pressed grey trousers.

'At times, when the south-easter blows, the mist settles on the mountain and pushes down this side. We call it the tablecloth.'

A pigeon settled on the table with a flutter of wings and Catherine fed it the last few crumbs of cake left on her plate.

'Adèle would love your country,' he said eventually, in the process of lighting a cigarette. 'Perhaps I shall bring her one day.'

'Your sister?' Catherine asked in surprise. 'Would you really bring her to South Africa?'

'Yes,' he replied, smiling. 'The two of you should get

on well. You are very much the same age. How old are you?' he asked, glancing at her speculatively. 'Eighteen? Nineteen, perhaps?'

'I'm twenty-two,' Catherine replied with such dignity that Paul could not help laughing. It was a relief as well to know that she was not as young as she appeared.

'My apologies, *chérie*. I would never have guessed it. Perhaps because I am so much older—'

'How old are you, Paul?' she interrupted, and then wondered that she had had the temerity to be so personal.

'Thirty-five, Catherine,' he replied without hesitation. 'Thirteen years older than you. It is almost a lifetime, no?'

'No!' she replied emphatically. 'Age means nothing when—'

'When two people are in love? Were you going to say that, *chérie*?' he asked, amused. 'But then we are not in love. You are not in love with me, are you, Catherine?'

'Of course not!' she replied as the tell-tale colour flooded her cheeks. Furious with herself for letting her tongue run away with her, she spoke more harshly than was necessary. 'Are all Frenchmen as frank and direct as yourself?'

'Not all,' Paul replied, his amusement replaced by a rueful expression. 'You must not believe all the stories you hear about the men in France. We are very much like other men all over the world.'

They sat in the shade of an oak tree with the sun streaming through the leaves and casting dappled shadows on the table. Paul wished that he could have lengthened his visit by a few weeks, but he had already remained longer than he had intended.

'You speak perfect English, Paul,' Catherine complimented him. 'Did you spend much time in England?'

'My mother was English,' he told her, crushing his cigarette in the ashtray. 'I went to university there. That is also where I met David Marsden.'

This information surprised Catherine, and she wondered why she had not realized before that they were old friends. It was obvious now when she thought of the way they had often addressed each other.

'Do you always stay away from the clinic for long periods such as this when you have a patient elsewhere?' she asked finally.

'Not always,' Paul smiled, finding her directness enchanting. 'I have taken a long-overdue holiday, and besides, the staff are excellently trained to continue without my presence.'

During the remainder of Paul's stay they visited the Castle, steeped in history dating back to 1666, but Paul was entranced by Groot Constantia, which was an excellent example of old Cape Dutch style houses. Once again it had its own history attached to it, having been granted to Simon van der Stel who was Governor of the Cape at the time.

'After his death in 1712,' Catherine informed Paul as they were admiring the old stinkwood furniture in the drawing-room, 'Groot Constantia changed hands many times and eventually became an experimental farm. It was damaged by fire in 1925 and had to be carefully reconstructed.'

Paul lovingly fingered a circular rosewood table. 'How is it that you know so much about all this?' He waved his arm about.

'I've come here often, and History was always my best subject at school,' she smiled. 'Especially the history of the Cape.'

Throughout these excursions to the various places of interest, Paul took great care that she should not overtax her strength, and called a halt whenever she showed signs of fatigue.

'This doctor with the fancy name,' Sarah said as they were preparing a picnic lunch on the morning prior to Paul's departure. 'When does he go back to his own country?'

Catherine shifted her walking stick from one hand to the other and placed a flask of coffee into the basket before replying.

'He leaves tomorrow, Sarah. Why?'

Sarah shrugged her shoulders. 'I just wondered, Miss Cathy. You've been out with him almost every day this week.'

Catherine leaned heavily on her stick as she watched Sarah rearrange the contents of the basket before closing the lid and fastening it securely. Despite the fact that she was exceedingly plump, her hands moved quickly and deftly, and Catherine, noticing the disapproving expression on her dark face, knew that these questions were leading up to something she would rather have avoided.

'You're in love with him, aren't you, Miss Cathy?' Sarah wiped her hands on her apron and stood facing Catherine with her hands on her hips. 'It's no use denying it either. It's written all over your face.'

'Sarah, I don't—'

'I've looked after you since the time your mother died. You were so small your nose didn't even touch the top of the table. I know you, Miss Cathy, I know the signs. You've been in love before, but this time you're loving the way a woman loves the only man in her life, with her heart, her mind and her soul.' One hand still resting on her hip, she raised the other and pointed a chubby finger at Catherine. 'But I warn you, Miss Cathy, you have heartache ahead of you. This doctor with the fancy name is a man who thinks with his head and not with his heart. He will never believe that you really love him and that you're not just being grateful for all he has done for you.'

'But—'

'*Ja*, he is very nice now, and pays a lot of attention to you,' Sarah continued firmly in her spicy English, 'but he can be a man without mercy when he thinks he's been cheated. I've seen him; I've watched him when he's been here to fetch you. And Miss Cathy, even Joseph agrees with me, the old rascal.'

Catherine took the weight off her trembling legs by subsiding weakly into a kitchen chair. 'Why are you saying all these things, Sarah?'

The elderly coloured girl walked around the table and placed a comforting hand on Catherine's shoulder, eyes alight with devotion. 'You'll have to fight for your happiness, Miss Cathy. You'll have to be patient, but in the end you'll find what you've been wanting most – the love and trust of the man you have chosen.'

When the front door bell chimed lustily, Catherine hastened to answer it and found Paul standing on the doorstep with a bunch of delicate pink roses in his hands.

'For you, *mademoiselle*,' he said, bowing slightly as he handed them to her.

Catherine lowered her head and inhaled the sweet fragrance emitting from the delicate blooms.

'Thank you, Paul, they're beautiful,' she smiled, and breaking off a perfect bud, she slipped it into the buttonhole of his jacket.

His eyes appraised her, taking in her colourful silk blouse, comfortable slacks and low-heeled sandals. Noticing her discomfort under his direct scrutiny, he smiled suddenly as Catherine, hastily turned and entered the house to place the roses in a vase. She was not averse to his glances and the attention he lavished upon her, Paul realized, yet their association had been too brief for him to ascertain whether her feelings stemmed purely from gratitude, or whether they went deeper.

As they drove into the country a short while later, Sarah's words echoed strangely through Catherine's mind. They intrigued, puzzled and frightened her. But in Paul's charming company she was able to shift her troubled thoughts to the recesses of her mind to ponder about at a later date.

They spent the morning driving through the Franschhoek valleys, visiting the wine cellars and walking through the vineyards. Finally, hungry and tired, they headed for a picnic spot along the banks of the Eerste River. It was a hot, sultry afternoon and the cicadas shrilled loudly as Catherine and Paul spread a blanket beneath a shady tree and ate their picnic lunch in silence.

Paul sat with his back resting against a tree trunk drinking his coffee. His white shirt was unbuttoned almost to the waist and from his neck hung a crucifix which nestled amongst the smattering of dark hair on his tanned, muscular chest. His shirt spanned tightly across his shoulders and the muscles in his arms rippled with each movement. He looked far too athletic to be a doctor, Catherine decided, yet when she observed his hands, she knew differently. His fingers were long and slender and she had experienced their supple strength many times during her convalescence.

She stretched herself out on the rug and wished the day would linger on for ever. They had discussed many things during the past few days, but his imminent departure was never mentioned. It was almost as though they had both been avoiding the subject, although it was ever present in Catherine's thoughts, taunting her almost to the point of desperation. Nothing would ever be the same again. Not after meeting a man like Paul de Meillon!

'Tell me about the Clinic,' she asked, rolling over on to her stomach and plucking nervously at a blade of grass.

Paul placed his empty cup in the basket and joined her on the rug. Propping himself up on one elbow, he stared out across the river, and she knew instinctively that his thoughts were not with her at that moment. She was excluded from that part of his life to which he would return the following day. After a few weeks she would no doubt be forgotten. Unhappiness flooded her being and left her strangely listless.

'What would you like to know, *petite*?'

'As much as you wish to tell me.'

'The neuro-clinic is situated on the outskirts of Paris,' he said eventually, his voice low and pleasant to her ears. 'We admit patients with various types of nervous disorders. Some of them are operative, others are not. My home is but a short distance from the Clinic, which is convenient, if not always practical.'

'Does your sister live with you?'

'During the holidays, *oui*. It is her home. But,' he smiled happily, 'from the end of this year she will be home for always. She will have completed her schooling in England and has decided to open a boutique in Paris. She is mad about clothes and fashions.'

'She sounds interesting,' Catherine mused, trying to imagine a girl with Paul's dark good looks. 'Has she money of her own with which to start a business of this nature?'

47

'A great deal of money has been left in my care for her until she turns twenty-one,' Paul admitted, taking his eyes off the scenery and looking down at her. 'You think this strange, that situations like this still occur? Perhaps you think it old-fashioned?'

'Not at all,' Catherine said hastily. 'Here in South Africa a girl still needs the consent of a parent or guardian to get married when she's under twenty-one."

'Ah! That is so!' he exclaimed. 'Adèle cannot marry unless I consider her chosen husband suitable.'

There was such finality in his voice that Catherine glanced at him quickly, noticing the grim expression on his normally calm features.

'Are you a very strict brother and guardian?'

'When I have to be, *chérie*,' he replied bluntly. 'But enough! It is time now that you tell me something about yourself.'

Catherine twined a blade of grass around her finger. 'There's nothing much to tell. I was at university studying for my B.Litt., and but for the accident I would have taken my final exams last year.'

'You can now return to your studies this year, since you are quite well again.'

'I don't think so,' The blade of grass snapped between her agitated fingers. 'I've been a millstone around my father's neck long enough. It's time I went out and made a living for myself.'

'Your father is a wealthy man, *chérie*. I am sure he does not mind your being a – millstone, as you put it.'

'I'm not that kind of girl, Paul,' she said, sitting up and brushing the hair out of her eyes. 'I have to be doing something. I either have to go back to my studies, or find myself a job of some sort. I'm not prepared to sit back for the rest of my life by just being

48

wealthy Charles Anderson's daughter. I'm a person in my own right, after all.'

There was approval in Paul de Meillon's dark eyes, and something more which Catherine could not quite define. She had not intended to say as much as she had, but it had all burst forth from a heart filled with the agonizing knowledge that, while she desired nothing more than to spend the rest of her life close to him, he in turn desired, obviously, nothing more than to be allowed to return to his beloved clinic in France. It was damnable!

She had been a fool to give her heart so freely, and above all, to someone who had no desire to have any part of it. Would he ever give his heart to anyone? she wondered. Would there ever come a time when his work would no longer give him enough satisfaction; a time when he would seek fulfilment elsewhere? With a woman, perhaps?

The thought made her cringe inwardly. The mere idea of another woman in his arms, receiving his kisses and whispered endearments, was too distressing to dwell upon.

They arrived back at De Rust late that afternoon as the last rays of the sun cast long pointed shadows across the earth, and bathed the mountain in a golden brilliance that took one's breath away. A cool breeze was blowing and the sweet perfume of the tuberoses filled the night air to render a poignant sadness about this moment of parting.

Catherine would have been immensely overjoyed had she been able to see into the heart of Paul de Meillon at that moment. Never had he been so loath to part from anyone as he was to part from this girl whom he loved so deeply.

He could have spoken, he knew, yet something had

held him back. She was young and needed time. The success of the operation he had performed was still too fresh in her memory for her to be able to distinguish between love and gratitude. Gratitude! The word made him cringe inwardly. Perhaps he was being too careful, but at his age a man could not afford to take chances when choosing a wife.

No, Paul decided. He must return to France and leave the way open for her to associate with other young men, no matter how distasteful the mere thought of this was to him, or what pain this parting would bring.

Within a year he would return and, if she was still free, he would then court her as a man courts the woman he loves. Perhaps then she will not be influenced by anything other than the language of her own heart.

'Catherine, *chérie*,' Paul began, taking her hands in his. 'I have made shameful use of your hospitality. You were not yet well enough for all this travelling around, and I am afraid that at times it must have tired you.'

'No, no! I've enjoyed every moment of it. After spending six months on your back and in a wheelchair, it was pure heaven to be able to walk about again.' Wild horses would not have dragged the confession from Catherine that she had suffered any discomfort at any time. She had been determined that nothing would mar the last few days they would have together. She lowered her eyes before his intensive gaze. 'I haven't yet thanked you for all you did for me. If it hadn't been for you—'

'There are others, *petite*,' he interrupted distastefully, 'who would have done the same for you had I not been here.'

'Who, for instance? David Marsden? He is the best neuro-surgeon we have in the country, and even he was not prepared to take the risk.'

'Do not think badly of my colleague, Catherine,' Paul reprimanded gently, placing a finger beneath her chin and tilting her face upwards. 'It is not easy for a man to operate on the woman he loves.'

Catherine's eyes widened. 'You can't be serious!'

'I assure you that I am, *chérie*. When I am gone, give him a chance, and think kindly of him.'

'But I don't—' Catherine bit back her words. It would be useless explaining that there was not the slightest chance of her ever falling in love with David Marsden, unless she was prepared to reveal her true feelings in the process.

'You will do this for me?'

'I can promise nothing, Paul. At the moment I feel nothing more than friendship for David, and quite frankly, I don't think it will ever be any different. He's my doctor, and that's all.'

Paul raised her hand to his lips. 'Take care of yourself, *chérie*. Do not overdo things for some time yet. You would not, I am sure, want to undo all my hard work. You will promise me this?'

'I promise, Paul.' She caught her trembling lip between her teeth. 'I – will you be paying us a visit again in the near future?'

'Perhaps, *petite*. Who knows?'

The breeze lifted her scarf from her neck and blew it against him. He caught it smartly, but when she held out her hand to retrieve it from him, he shook his head.

'I may keep it as a memento, *oui*?'

Stunned by this request, she was for a moment bereft of speech. She nodded slightly and watched him place it carefully in his jacket pocket. Why should he want a memento of her? she wondered confusedly. Did he then want to remember her for some reason? The rose she had given him hung limply against his jacket lapel. Without the life-giving water and soil, it had withered and died. She knew, too, that she would be as lifeless as that poor rose once Paul had gone, and the knowledge was not pleasant.

'I must leave you now, *mignonne*. It is getting late and there is still much packing to do.' Once again he lifted her hand and kissed her fingertips lightly. 'You have done me a service by showing me just a little of your beautiful country. I shall not forget it."

Then, unexpectedly, he bent his dark head and placed his lips against hers for a fraction of a second, Her whole being cried out for his arms to hold her, if only this once, close to his heart, but this was not to be. He stepped back and the moment was gone.

'My regards to your father. Perhaps, one day, you and I shall meet again. *Adieu*,' he said softly before turning on his heel and leaving her alone on the terrace with the bitter-sweet scent of tuberoses as her only comfort.

To Catherine it was the end of the world, but to Paul de Meillon? She wished she knew. Never once had she been able to glimpse his feelings or his thoughts. His manner towards her had been impeccable at all times, and if she had been foolish enough to fall in love with him, it certainly was not because he had encouraged her. He had been friendly and charming, but nothing more.

With tear-filled eyes she saw his car pass through the gates and disappear from view. A sob rose in her throat as utter desolation settled about her like a heavy cloak.

From an upstairs window Sarah watched sadly as Catherine entered the house.

'*Ja*,' she thought, shaking her head sorrowfully. 'It has happened, and the good Lord only knows where it will end. My poor Miss Cathy!'

CHAPTER FOUR

SUE GRAINGER'S parties had always been an experience not to be missed. Modern to her very fingertips, she had furnished her flat in the same manner. Weird paintings adorned the walls while chairs covered with the most outrageously coloured material had been placed at strategic points to lend a futuristic atmosphere to an otherwise rather bare lounge.

Catherine had arrived early as Sue had suggested. They had much to talk about considering the many months Catherine had been out of circulation. More than that, Sue was anxious to show off her newly acquired flat.

Now, as the room was steadily becoming more and more crowded, Catherine wedged herself into a corner close to the door leading on to the balcony, and surveyed her surroundings with a certain amount of alarm. It was extraordinary to think that less than a year ago she had taken such an active part in parties similar to this. Young men with beards, long hair, and the most repulsive taste in clothes propped themselves up against the walls or furniture, while the girls, dressed in similar style, appeared to be ranking all over them.

From Sue's hi-fi set the throbbing rhythm of the music reverberated through the room until Catherine's temples throbbed in unison. Clinging couples swayed together on the floor in the dim light as Catherine sent a searching glance across the room to where Sue was locked in the embrace of her current boy-friend. She and Sue had been friends since their schooldays, and yet they had such vastly different natures. Sue had always been fun, yet tonight Catherine found her somewhat disgusting.

'Well, well, look who's here!'

Catherine looked up in surprise to find Ronnie Jansen, the inevitable drink in his hand, standing beside her chair. She had not seen him arrive, yet she should have known that he was as much a part of Sue's parties as Sue herself. 'Hello, Ronnie.'

'Hello, Ronnie,' he mocked. 'Just like that! As though you've been seeing me every day of your life.'

'What did you expect me to say?' she asked sarcastically. 'Fancy meeting you here?'

'Not exactly, after all, that old cliché is rather worn out by now,' he remarked, seating himself on the arm of her chair. 'You couldn't perhaps be a little more original?'

'I should have known you would be here,' Catherine remarked. 'You rarely missed one of Sue's parties in the past.'

'Is that why you came tonight?'

'Just as conceited as ever, aren't you?' she quipped back.

'What has happened to your bodyguard?'

'Bodyguard?' Catherine was floundering for a moment, and then she understood. 'I presume you mean Dr. de Meillon?'

Ronnie shrugged. 'Who else?'

'He's gone back to France,' she replied stiffly.

'Shame, so the little girl is all on her own tonight,' he grinned distastefully, as he slipped an arm about her which she evaded smartly by vacating her chair. 'All right! You can't blame a chap for trying, can you? No need to recoil from me as if I have a contagious disease. I get the message, sweetie, and I won't bother you

55

again. Who wants a cold fish for a girl-friend, anyhow?'

With that he slid off the chair and moved to the other side of the room while Catherine sat down once more with a certain amount of relief that he had left her in peace so readily.

She tried to imagine Paul de Meillon at a party of this nature, and knew beyond doubt that there would be a look of disapproval on his face as he looked about him. Yes, that was exactly the emotion Catherine was experiencing at that moment. Disapproval! What kind of girl had she been to have found these wild parties enjoyable? For the first time she was thankful that the accident had put an end to this side of her life. It had been a mistake to come, but Sue had been so insistent, and her father had thought that it might cheer her up to a certain extent, for since Paul's departure she had been restless and unhappy. The futility of her emotions depressed her and left her listless and unable to decide about her future.

Her headache increased with every minute as the music grew louder and wilder. When the opportunity arose she hurried over to Sue, made her excuses and left, breathing in the cool and refreshing night air as she drove home.

By the time she reached De Rust she had resolved never to attend another of Sue's parties. Their friendship, if one could call it that, was at an end. The difference in their characters had driven them too far apart to ever recapture their earlier relationship.

'You're home early,' her father observed as she entered the house.

'I developed a slight headache,' she explained, bending down to plant a kiss on his forehead.

Charles Anderson laid his book aside and looked

closely at his daughter. 'Did something happen to upset you?'

Catherine kicked off her shoes and poured herself a fruit drink. 'Nothing has upset me, Daddy. I suddenly realized that I've outgrown Sue's parties like so many other things I used to find exciting,' she replied, curling up in a chair opposite him. 'How was your evening?'

'The meeting ended quite early, so I've spent most of the evening sitting here reading.' He lit himself a cigarette. 'David Marsden telephoned while you were out?'

'Oh?' Her interest quickened. 'Did he say what he wanted?'

'No. He merely said I was to ask you to have lunch with him tomorrow. If you can't make it you should telephone him, otherwise you're to meet him at the Cabana restaurant at one o'clock.'

Catherine wondered what this strange request was all about. She and David had become close friends during the past few weeks, and although he made it obvious that he wanted more than friendship, he was nevertheless pleasant company, and never once forced himself upon her.

'You've been seeing quite a lot of David Marsden lately,' Charles remarked casually.

'Yes, I have.'

'Is there ... I mean ...' His sentence, though unfinished, was eloquent enough and Catherine could not help laughing at his discomfiture.

'No, there isn't, Daddy,' she assured him. 'I'm very fond of David, but that's all.'

'Does he feel the same way about you?'

She hesitated a moment. This was the only thing that marred their friendship. 'David is in love with me, Daddy. He realizes that I don't feel the same way about him, and he accepts the fact.'

'But are you being fair to the chap by continually going out with him?' her father persisted.

Catherine's green eyes widened innocently. 'Am I to refuse his invitations, then?'

Charles Anderson shifted uncomfortably in his chair. 'I didn't say that, Cathy. Heaven knows you go out little enough lately, and I can't begrudge you the time you spend with him. What I'm getting at is that it's rather hard on a fellow when he happens to be in love with a woman, and she doesn't reciprocate his feelings.'

She considered this for a moment in earnest. 'You're right, Daddy. It isn't fair, but it's going to be difficult convincing David that it's for his own good.' She sighed heavily, slipping off the chair. 'I'm off to bed, I'm rather tired this evening. Good night, Daddy.'

Long after she had left him, Charles remained seated staring thoughtfully in front of him. He was worried about Catherine. She was not herself lately, and appeared to withdraw completely from all gaiety; even from himself, her own father. What had caused this change in her, he did not know, but he was determined to find out.

When Catherine arrived at the Cabana restaurant the following day at one o'clock, David was there waiting for her. He took her to a quiet table in the corner and ordered drinks while they waited for their meal to be served.

'You mentioned some time ago that you'd applied to return to university in order to complete your final year,' David remarked as they sat sipping at their aperitifs. 'Do you still want to go back?'

'Yes, David, I do.'

David nodded thoughtfully. 'I saw the Dean of the university last night, and he told me that your application had been accepted. Apparently you'll be hearing from them shortly as they want you to return as soon as possible.'

For the first time in weeks Catherine felt a little thrill of excitement quiver through her. At last she would be able to do something constructive. She would have to work hard, and through her work she might be able to forget. Forget that there ever was such a man as Paul de Meillon.

'Cathy,' David interrupted her thoughts, 'you don't have to go back to university, you know.'

'You're not suggesting that I spend the rest of my life doing absolutely nothing, are you?'

He leaned across the tables and covered her hand with his own. 'You could marry me, Cathy. You know I love you, don't you?'

For several seconds their eyes met and held. His were passionate; hers apologetic. 'I know you love me, David,' she murmured gently, 'but—'

'You could learn to love me in time,' he persisted, and Catherine smiled whimsically. How easy it would have been if that were true! David was not unattractive, with his fair hair and grey eyes that crinkled at the corners when he smiled, but there stood between them the compelling figure of a dark-haired French surgeon. Catherine shook herself slightly as she concentrated on the man seated opposite her.

'It wouldn't be any use, David, my dear. I don't – I can't . . .' Her voice trailed off into silence. It was not easy to hurt someone the way she was hurting David at that moment.

'Is there someone else?' he probed, his disappointment clearly written on his face.

For a moment she could not answer, then she nodded slowly. 'Yes, there is. I'm sorry.'

'Someone I know?'

'Yes.'

'Not – not Paul de Meillon!' he exclaimed. Then, as he read the truth in her eyes, he released her hand and sat back in his chair with a grim expression on his handsome face. 'So it *is* him. I should have known.'

'I'm sorry, David,' she said once more, inadequately.

He drained his glass as their meal arrived, and for a while they ate in silence. 'You realize, of course, that loving Paul is quite a futile occupation,' he said eventually with a trace of bitterness in his voice. 'He's married to his profession. Always has been, and always will be.'

He had no way of knowing how wrong that assumption of his was, and neither had Catherine, as she pushed her fork idly through her food. Her appetite had long since deserted her, but for David's sake she made a pretence of eating.

'I know all this, David. I knew from the first moment I met Paul that there was no place for a woman in his life,' she told him bitterly. 'He's by no means immune to women, but once his interest has waned, then he has no further use for them.'

'Then why, in heaven's name ...!' he exploded, unable to finish what he was about to say.

'Why did I go and do a foolish thing like falling in love with him?' she concluded for him. A little nerve fluttered at the corner of her mouth. 'I don't know, David. I didn't want to. God knows I didn't want to love him, but ... it just happened, and there was nothing I could do about it. It's there, and nothing in this world could eradicate it.'

Tears brimmed in her eyes and she blinked rapidly. How silly! She had been so sure that she had got over that tearful stage, and here she was on the verge of tears once more, and in public of all places.

David gripped her hand across the table and squeezed it comfortingly. 'I'm sorry, Cathy. I didn't want to make you cry.'

'Oh, please, I'm just being silly. It will pass in time, this feeling of helpless futility.'

When David eventually walked with her to her car, she was quite composed.

'Does Paul know? he asked suddenly as he helped her into her car.

'No! Good heavens, he must never know!' she replied agitatedly.

'Don't worry, Cathy. I shan't be the one to tell him. Besides, we very seldom correspond, and when we do it normally has to do with our job, which makes our letters rather brief and to the point.' He bent down and placed a hand over hers at the wheel. 'Please remember, Cathy, that I'm always there if you should need me. We can still be friends, can't we?'

A slow smile lit up her face. 'Yes, my dear, we can still be friends,' she agreed. 'And thank you for asking me to have lunch with you.'

David stood aside as Catherine pulled away from the kerb and drove homeward.

The year passed with surprising speed for Catherine. Once back at university, there was no time to sit and brood about her own problems as she was instantly swept up in the hive of activity amongst the other students. Along with several others, she had managed to find herself a job during the holidays to earn some extra money — not that she needed it, for Charles Anderson was a wealthy man, but Catherine needed to be occupied.

On graduation day her father and David Marsden were present when she received her degree. It had been a joyous occasion that lingered on until the evening, when the three of them had dinner at a restaurant on the beach-front.

'I have a surprise for you, Cathy,' her father told her as they lingered over their coffee. 'You'll have to wait until we get home, though.'

'What is it, Daddy?' she inquired excitedly, then, glancing at David, she asked: 'Do you know about this surprise?'

'I do,' he admitted laughingly, 'but don't for one moment think I'm going to tell you what it is.'

'I think you're both being quite horrible,' she pouted playfully.

'Yes, I know we're monsters,' her father agreed, smiling with satisfaction, 'but the surprise will have to wait until we are alone at home. You're invited to come along as well, David,' her father added, winking at him.

Later, while driving home, Catherine could hardly contain her curiosity. Whatever the surprise was, she was certain it had been contrived between her father and David. They behaved like two schoolchildren who were cherishing a secret and were unable to suppress the occasional giggle.

'Well,' Charles Anderson said dramatically once they were all three settled in the magnificently furnished living-room at De Rust. 'Now for the surprise I promised you, Cathy.'

From the drawer of the old Victorian writing bureau he extracted an envelope and handed it to Catherine.

Trembling with suppressed excitement, she held the slightly bulky envelope for a moment longer, wondering what the contents could be. Then, with a somewhat jerky movement, she slit it open and extracted the contents.

Her expressive eyes widened as she held the documents in her hands. 'Why, it's two tickets for an overseas trip!'

'That's right. For me it will be a business-cum-holiday trip, but for you it will be merely a holiday.'

For one wild moment Catherine thought of Paul, then, thrusting her thoughts aside, she flung her arms around her father's neck and kissed him excitedly.

'Daddy, you're an absolute darling!' she cried laughingly. 'I've always wanted to go to Europe and now, just like that, it's all arranged!'

David Marsden, who had been standing quietly by, stepped forward then and placed a friendly arm about Catherine's shoulders. 'Both your father and I feel that you deserve this holiday more than anything else he could give you of material value. You've worked hard this year, and last year it was the accident which drained you of vitality.' He kissed her lightly on the cheek. 'I hope you both enjoy yourselves as you should.'

'I think you've both been extremely kind to think of me in this way, and I want you to know that I appreciate it tremendously. I – I—' The tears of joy were close as she bit her trembling lip to steady it.

Charles cleared his throat. 'You're going to have to start packing, my girl. We haven't much time, you know.'

'Do you realize,' she laughed, 'I've been so excited that I never even looked at the date of our departure.'

'We're leaving the day after tomorrow,' Charles told her. 'December isn't exactly the best time to go to Europe, so you'd better make sure that you pack enough warm clothes for yourself.'

'Good heavens!' she exclaimed. 'I *will* have to rush, won't I? What about your clothes, Daddy?'

'Don't worry about mine,' he laughed, 'Sarah has been doing some packing for me when you weren't about.'

'You rascal, Daddy!' she cried excitedly, hugging him once more.

'Which countries will you be visiting?' David asked, relaxing in his armchair.

Catherine looked at her father expectantly.

'Oh, well,' he replied, offering David a cigarette and lighting one for himself, 'we're starting off with Italy, and then going on to Switzerland where we shall be spending Christmas. From there we shall go to Germany, France, Spain, and then England. We might not be visiting them in quite that order as I have a few business appointments to keep,' he explained, 'but we shall nevertheless visit as many countries as possible.'

'How long will you be away?' David asked, glancing at Catherine, and she knew instinctively that he was not very happy about their intended trip despite the wonderful show he was putting on.

Charles puffed at his cigarette. 'About two months, I should say.'

Once again David's glance met hers searchingly, and Catherine wished with all her heart that she could have loved this wonderful man enough to have married him. She lowered her eyes and fiddled self-consciously with the catch of her bracelet.

'I must be off,' David said after a moment, rising to

his feet. 'It's been a long and tiring day for you, Cathy. I suggest you go to bed now, because tomorrow is going to be an equally tiring day, what with getting everything ready for your trip.'

'Yes, you're right,' she nodded, smiling up at him. 'I'll do just what my doctor orders me to do,' she added playfully.

'You do that,' David said with mock severity, as they walked with him to the door.

'Shall we see you again before we leave, David?' Charles asked as they stepped on to the terrace.

'I'll come and see you off at the airport.'

'Good. I'll say good night, then,' Charles said before re-entering the house and leaving them alone for a few moments.

The crickets chirped loudly from the dark recesses of the garden as they stood in silence facing each other, each of them loath to bid the other good-night.

David stepped forward suddenly and placed his hands on either side of her face. 'Cathy, let's become engaged before you leave for Europe. Please?'

The suddenness of this suggestion caught Catherine unawares and for a moment the question hung heavily between them, until she heaved a shuddering sigh. 'David, my dear, you know that I love you dearly as a friend. It would break my heart if I became engaged to you now, and then had to break it off at some future date.'

'But, Cathy—'

'Let's rather wait,' she interrupted beseechingly. 'Let's wait until I return from this trip. Perhaps . . . who can tell . . .' she ended lamely, the tears brimming her eyes.

David released her and she turned away from him, placing her forehead against the cool stone pillar.

'Are you still in love with Paul?'

Yes. Paul de Meillon. She had thought of him that evening as well, but only for a moment.

'It's strange that you should ask that question,' she replied slowly, turning to face him in the darkness. 'Am I still in love with Paul? I really don't know. Ten months is a long time, and so much has happened since that brief period we knew each other.'

'Well, then?' David persisted, stepping closer to her.

Catherine sensed that her statement had given him new hope and she knew that she must quell it instantly.

'David, I'm not sure any more. During these past months I've tried to analyse my feelings and have often wondered if it hadn't merely been a deep sense of gratitude which I mistook for love. I tell you, I don't know,' she cried in desperation. 'I'm only sure of the fact that I loved him then – desperately! The activities at the university left me very little time to ponder over my own problems. What I shall feel like when I see him again, *if* I should ever see him again, I really don't know. It may just be like meeting an old friend again, I suppose.' She laughed unsteadily. 'Why are we talking like this? I shan't be seeing Paul at all. In the first place, he doesn't know that we're going to be in France some time in the future, and in the second place, I'm certainly not going to go running after him.'

'Cathy,' David said seriously, tilting her face upwards, 'promise me one thing. If you should see Paul, and you find that you have nothing left of your old feeling for him, will you then seriously consider my proposal of marriage?'

'David, I—'

'Will you?' he insisted, taking her by the shoulders

and shaking her slightly.

She considered this for a moment. What harm could it do, after all, to make such a promise? 'Yes, David, I will do as you ask, but please – please don't expect too much of me,' she begged.

He kissed her lightly on the lips. 'I shall be waiting, Cathy. Waiting and hoping.'

Before Catherine could reply, David had turned and was hurrying down the steps towards his car. Long after he had left she still stood staring thoughtfully into the darkness. Was she just being a fool, she asked herself, not to accept David's proposal? She would certainly not lack in material comfort as his wife, but . . . would it be fair to him? Would his love be enough for both of them? And, how long would he be satisfied with a wife who did not love him as it was his right to be loved? And yet . . . she was fond of him. Yes, she was extremely fond of David Marsden. He was a darling, but could she love him?

Catherine sighed unhappily and wandered inside. She was tired, excited and distressed at the same time. So much had happened that day – the thrill of achievement at receiving her degree, the excitement of their planned trip, and now the unhappiness of having to hurt David. It had all been too much for her.

She locked the front door and snapped off the hall light. Tomorrow was going to be a rush, she thought, but it was going to be fun.

Catherine strolled along the Champs Elysées in Paris with the delightful feeling of anticipation tingling in her veins. It was January, and winter in Europe, yet not even the cold could diminish her fascination for the countries they had visited. She was at a loose end that afternoon while her father spent time with a business associate. On other occasions she had accompanied him, but on this delightful afternoon she could not bear the thought of spending hours chatting idly to strangers while her father was ensconced in a room somewhere talking shop.

Turning up the collar of her coat as the cold nipped her ears, she walked along admiring the street cafés with their gaily coloured awnings. In spite of the freezing weather many people still frequented these cafés, and she was thinking of persuading her father to have tea with her there some time.

Ahead of her was the Arc de Triomphe and a little to her left, the Eiffel Tower stood towering above the city. An ecstatic sigh escaped past her lips. Strange, she thought as she looked about her – to these people going about their business, it was just a city like any other, but to her it was almost unreal in its beauty. A singular city steeped in history which led to revolution and bloodshed, and which had nevertheless maintained its enchantment.

The traffic was increasing steadily as she glanced at her watch. It was getting late and she would have to take a taxi to the Hotel Boulevard if she wanted to reach it before dinner, she decided.

Once at the hotel, she bathed and changed into a warm evening dress. Her father had not arrived yet, the desk clerk had informed her, so there was ample time to prepare for dinner. As Catherine put the finishing touches to her make-up, her thoughts drifted back to the moment they had boarded the plane at D.F. Malan Airport.

Their flight had already been called when David came rushing towards them. He had been delayed and could not make it earlier. He shook her father's hand vigorously and then, for the first time, pulled her into his arms. He had kissed her passionately, almost desperately, before releasing her. Taken aback, and acutely aware of the fact that her father had witnessed this passionate farewell, she blushed and stammered her good-bye. Their flight was called a second time, and hurriedly they had boarded the plane that would take them first to Italy.

It had been a wonderful holiday so far, she thought as she stared through the window at the Eiffel Tower in the distance. From Italy they had gone on to Spain, then to Switzerland and Germany. They took their time visiting the places of interest and moved on to the next country when they began to feel restless. It was in Germany that they decided to visit France as a last stop before going to England, and then home.

Although it was winter in Paris, nothing could deprive the city of the enchantment it held for her. South Africa, at that moment, seemed a long way away, as indeed it was.

The shrill ring of the telephone interrupted her thoughts and, thinking it was her father, she hurried across the room to answer it.

'Room 209.'

'*Salut, chérie*, and welcome to Paris.'

For a moment Catherine was stunned into silence and almost dropped the receiver as she heard those deep tones at the other end of the line.

'Paul!'

She leaned back against the wall as the blood coursed wildly through her veins, leaving her strangely numb.

'I am surprised that you recognized my voice after all this time.'

'I know of no one else here in Paris who would have the audacity to call me *chérie*,' she replied, grateful that

69

he could not see her flushed cheeks and quivering hands. 'Where are you telephoning from?'

'From the foyer of this hotel,' he told her. 'I met your father quite by chance this afternoon at the home of Monsieur Berton and he invited me to have dinner with you.'

'Oh.' Stunned by the effect his voice was having on her nervous system, she could find nothing else to say.

'He says I am to tell you that he gives you five minutes to get down here to the lounge,' Paul continued.

'Tell him I'm stretching his five minutes to ten, and if he complains, remind him of all the times I have had to wait for him,' she replied, glancing down at her long evening gown, and mentally choosing something more appropriate to wear.

'I will do that, *chérie*,' Paul laughed. '*Au revoir*.'

There was a click as the line went dead.

For a few seconds Catherine stared at the receiver in her hand as though it was something she had never seen before. Paul was here! In this very hotel! She had thought she would never see him again and had managed to persuade herself that what she had felt for him had been nothing more than a deep gratitude. Yet here she was, quivering with excitement at the mere sound of his voice, while the feelings she had thought dead and buried were very much alive and vibrant.

Hastily she went through her wardrobe and selected a dark green evening gown which would be both warm and elegant. Hurriedly she changed, and then stood for a moment inspecting herself in the full-length mirror. The cut of the gown was superb and afforded her the amount of sophistication and confidence she needed. She hastily dabbed some powder on her nose and, satisfied with her reflection, picked up her evening bag and wrap before leaving the room.

Taking the lift down to the ground floor, she felt her pulse rate quicken alarmingly. Surely she was not afraid to meet Paul again? Nonsense, she told herself, and put it down to the fact that she had rushed.

Minutes later she stepped into the foyer and walked towards the lounge. She spotted her father immediately as she entered and then ... Paul. Tall, dark and immensely attractive in a dark evening suit, he at once stepped forward to meet her, a smile lighting up his lean features. The heavy beat of her heart was pounding in her ears as he took her extended hand and raised it to her lips.

'You are looking well, *chérie*, and more beautiful than I remembered.'

'You flatter me, Paul, but thank you.' She raised her eyes to his and felt herself blush as his glance swept over her before returning once more to her face.

'I do not flatter you, Catherine, I speak the truth. Come,' he took her arm and led her to the table, 'sit down while I order us a drink before we leave for the restaurant.'

Catherine planted a kiss on her father's cheek and sat down as Paul called the waiter and ordered aperitifs.

'How long will you be staying in France?' Paul asked eventually.

'I'm not sure. A few days, perhaps longer.' Charles glanced questioningly at Catherine. 'It all depends on Cathy.'

'You have seen much of our charming city?' Paul then asked her.

'I haven't seen much at all. We only arrived yesterday and since then I've been following Daddy around

71

and doing window-shopping while he attended to some business.'

'Then you must allow me to be your guide,' Paul offered instantly. 'I extend this invitation to you as well, *monsieur*,' he added, turning to Charles.

'Oh, good heavens, I'm too old to go charging about all over the place. But you take Cathy by all means.'

'You do not mind, *monsieur*?' Paul asked with raised eyebrows.

'Not at all.'

Later, while they were enjoying an after-dinner liqueur in the restaurant Paul had suggested, he got to his feet and extended his hand towards Catherine.

'Come, *chérie*, the musicians are excelling themselves this evening.'

Catherine hid her nervousness behind a smile as she placed her hand in his and walked on to the floor with him. There were several couples dancing to the dreamy melody the band was playing as Paul guided her amongst them with ease. He was a superb dancer, she discovered, as their steps matched with remarkable ease, and soon she was lost in the magic of the moment.

His arm closed about her slender waist more firmly as he held her closer to him.

'You have not spoken much this evening, *chérie*,' he said, bending his head so that his lips were level with her ear. 'Although I find your silence charming, I am also curious to know what thoughts are going round in that pretty head of yours.'

'Very uninteresting thoughts, Paul, I promise you,' she replied, lowering her lashes. He would be alarmed if he knew what a devastating effect his nearness had on her treacherous heart.

'Let me be the judge of that,' he ordered firmly.

'I – I—' Her steps faltered and she bit her lip. 'I'm sorry. I—'

'Come,' he interrupted. 'Let us get some air, and at the same time we can talk. I see your good father is engrossed in conversation with the charming lady at the table beside ours, so he will not miss us for a few moments.'

Paul guided her on to the terrace, and unused to the chilly European evenings, Catherine shivered sudenly.

'Here,' he said, instantly removing his jacket and placing it about her shoulders. 'I am used to this weather,' he told her as she was about to protest.

The warmth of his body still clung to the jacket and she felt a thrill go through her as if he had touched her physically.

'What have you been doing these past months?' he asked, as they seated themselves on a stone bench.

The lights of Paris flickered, filling her with the same feeling of anticipation she had experienced that afternoon during her walk. There was something about Paris that touched her soul, and reached out to her with invisible hands.

'I went back to university and got my degree,' she replied, watching him light a cigarette. The flame of his lighter gave a harshness to his lean face that was unkind.

'Ah!' He exhaled the smoke into the night air. 'I wondered if you would do so.'

The pearl buttons on his white shirt-front gleamed in the light the restaurant shed on to the terrace. He stretched forth a hand and took her left hand in his, holding it up for inspection.

'I see you are not wearing an engagement ring. Has my good friend David not yet persuaded you to marry him?'

Catherine looked down at her hand in his as though it was some strange object she had never seen before. 'We're good friends, that's all.'

'But surely he has asked you to marry him?' he persisted.

She looked away, avoiding the direct scrutiny of his dark eyes. They saw so much, too much, and if there was one thing she would not let him see, it was what really lay in her heart.

'Yes, he has,' she admitted eventually, 'but . . .' Her voice trailed off into silence.

'You do not love him?'

'No.'

'A pity,' he said softly, and yet there was something in his voice that made her realize that he did not think it a pity at all. Her heart leapt as she self-consciously released her hand from his.

'Your sister Adèle,' she changed the subject. 'Did she start her boutique as she had wanted to?'

'So you remembered!' he exclaimed with pleasure. 'Yes, she did. And she is doing very well. You must meet her while you are here.'

'I would like to very much.'

'*Bon*!'

The music stopped and Catherine returned his jacket as they went inside.

'Monsieur Anderson,' Paul said as they reached the table, 'I beg you to excuse me, but I have to visit a patient of mine and it takes a considerable time to reach the clinic. Thank you for asking me to join you this evening, it has been most enjoyable.' He turned to face Catherine, and smiled warmly. 'I will telephone you as soon as I have a free moment. *Bonne nuit, chérie, monsieur.*'

They bade him good night and he bowed and left. It was to Catherine as though the enchantment of the evening had departed with him. Picking up her wrap and her evening bag, she suggested to her father that they leave as well.

'I'm going up to bed, Daddy,' she said when they finally reached the hotel. 'See you in the morning.'

'See you in the morning,' he echoed, and watched her thoughtfully as she walked away from him.

Fate had decreed that Paul de Meillon's path should cross theirs once more, and Charles was at once hopeful and fearful for his daughter's happiness.

CHAPTER FIVE

The following evening when the telephone rang in Catherine's suite, she knew instinctively that it would be Paul as she hastened to answer it.

'I hope I am not telephoning at an inconvenient time,' he apologized. 'I have just this moment returned from the clinic.'

'Not at all,' she assured him hastily. 'I was sitting reading as it's too early to go to bed yet.'

'Have you planned anything for tomorrow?'

Catherine's heartbeats quickened. 'No. No, I haven't.'

'*Bon!* I have managed to arrange things at this end so that I shall be free tomorrow.' He hesitated a moment. 'Shall I call for you in the morning so that we can spend the day sightseeing?'

'Yes,' she replied quickly – too quickly. 'That would be lovely, Paul,' she added, blushing furiously and thankful that he could not see.

At the other end of the line, Paul smiled to himself as he heard the eagerness in her voice, and wondered how he would manage to pass the hours before he would see her again.

'What have you been doing today?' he asked.

'Daddy and I took a bus tour into the country,' she told him. 'We got back shortly before dinner.'

'Then you must be tired,' he said remorsefully, 'And here I am keeping you from going to bed.'

'No!' she denied hastily, unwilling for him to ring off so soon. It was heaven to hear his voice, and she savoured every moment of it as she cradled the receiver against her ear. 'I'm not at all tired, and most probably shan't be going to bed for ages yet.'

'You are very kind, *chérie*.' His voice was warm and vibrant and sent delicious little shivers up her spine. 'However, I must not keep you any longer. I will call for you at eight tomorrow morning. *Bonne nuit, chérie*.'

'Good night, Paul.'

On the outskirts of Paris, Paul sat in his book-lined study, his expression suddenly grim. He would have to be careful, he warned himself. She was attractive and charming, with the innocence of youth still upon her. It was obvious to him that she had not yet been awakened to love, and he would have to steel himself against rushing her off her feet. He had one innate fear and this was that, if he should ask her, she would marry him out of gratitude. He would demand more than gratitude from the woman he loved, and would therefore have to make very sure of her feelings before he plunged himself into the matrimonial state.

He lit a cigarette and drew the smoke deeply into his lungs. These past ten months had not been easy for him. He knew that David Marsden was in love with Catherine, and with each passing day he dreaded hearing the news that they were to be married. It was a chance he had had to take. The unexpected arrival in Paris of Catherine and her father had saved him a trip to South Africa which he had fully intended taking within the very near future. The express purpose of his visit would have been to visit Catherine in an effort to ascertain whether there was any hope for him.

Paul inhaled deeply on his cigarette once more, and frowned. *Le bon dieu* knew that he was not a patient man, but his fear that Catherine's decision might be influenced by her feeling of gratitude had given him the courage to continue with his plans. *Dieu!* It would be unbearable to discover after a time that she did not really care.

His meeting with Charles Anderson the previous afternoon had not been due to chance, as he had made them believe. Monsieur Berton's aged mother was a patient at the Clinic, and it was on one of Monsieur Berton's visits to his mother that they happened to discuss Paul's trip to South Africa the previous year. When Monsieur Berton mentioned that a Monsieur Anderson from South Africa had arranged a meeting with him, Paul had made a mental note to call on Monsieur Berton that day. The unexpected discovery that Catherine had accompanied her father on this trip had delighted Paul tremendously.

He crushed the remainder of his cigarette into an ashtray, and took his time selecting a book from the shelf. He would have to get through the night somehow if sleep evaded him.

Catherine awoke the following morning with a feeling of exhilaration. Not even the bleak winter sky could dampen her feelings. Humming softly to herself, she bathed and dressed with care at the prospect of spending the day sightseeing with Paul.

She selected an amber-coloured woollen dress which she had bought during a shopping excursion in Switzerland. It matched the coppery tints in her hair, and accentuated the green of her eyes. She had a quick breakfast of strong black coffee and a slice of buttered toast before hastening downstairs.

Paul, dressed in comfortable slacks, warm sweater and sports jacket, was entering the building as she reached the foyer. He smiled broadly when he saw her, displaying strong white teeth in his dark, handsome face, and Catherine felt her heart turn over at the sight of him.

A gleaming white Bentley was parked at the entrance, and he wasted no time with helping her into the comfortable interior. As he slid behind the wheel, he turned to her for a moment, a slight smile playing about his lips.

'I hope you are well prepared, *chérie*. It is going to be an exhausting day, for there is much to see and do.'

Catherine nodded breathlessly and, satisfied, Paul turned his attention to the traffic as they slid away from the kerb.

Paul had been right about the day being exhausting, for he took her on a whirlwind tour of the Louvre, Notre Dame and the Luxembourg Gardens. They went out in a rowing boat on the lake in the Bois de Boulogne, which was not advisable in winter, Paul had informed her, yet Catherine had insisted. After that excursion they travelled almost to the other side of the city once more to visit the Zoo, where she went into raptures at the sight of a swan swimming about on the lake, with two little cygnets in hot pursuit.

'You are enchanting, *mon enfant*,' Paul laughed as they sat down on a bench nearby. 'In these few hours I have given you a glimpse of the magnificence of Paris, and here you are completely enthralled at the sight of the swans. You have hurt my feelings, *ma petite*.'

'Oh, Paul, I'm sorry,' she breathed, quite ashamed of herself. 'I've seen so many impressive buildings today, and such impressive works of art, that my brain can't absorb any more. The restfulness of the swan with her young ones was so contrasting with what I've already seen that I couldn't help myself. Forgive me, please.'

She lifted her gold-tipped lashes and he looked down into the green depths of her eyes. His heart thudded uncomfortably. *Dieu*, how beautiful she was! So close was she to him that he had only to lower his head a fraction to taste the sweetness of her lips. *Ciel!* What was he thinking of? He did not want to frighten her. With the greatest effort he managed to regain control of his emotions.

Catherine felt as though she had been on the brink of a discovery. Those few seconds when their eyes had met and held had seemed like hours, during which she had become aware of a magnetism, drawing her closer to him. His eyes had been like two coals of fire, scorching her as they searched her very soul. There had been a moment when she had been almost sure he was about to kiss her, and she had waited breathlessly. Then something happened, and the moment was gone. She lowered her eyes while he busied himself lighting a cigarette.

'I was only teasing you, *chérie*,' he said, drawing deeply on his cigarette and turning to her. 'Do not look so alarmed.'

A tremulous smile quivered on her lips as she leaned back against the bench with a sigh. 'I thought, perhaps, you were angry with me.'

Paul took hold of the hand closest to his own and raised it to his lips. I could never be angry with you, *ma très chère*.'

'*Ma très chère*,' she echoed softly. 'What does it mean, Paul?'

'Perhaps, one day, I shall tell you,' he smiled briefly, releasing her hand. He finished his cigarette in silence and then crushed it under his heel. 'For how long do you intend staying in France?' he asked suddenly, stretching his legs out in front of him and pushing his hands into his trouser pockets.

'I'm not sure.' She hesitated. 'We were intending to leave again at the end of the week.'

A frown creased his brow. 'So soon?'

Catherine glanced at him quickly. 'Why do you ask, Paul?'

He turned to her slowly, placing his arm along the back of the bench behind her shoulders. His expression was calm and thoughtful as she waited for him to speak. 'Would you and your father care to extend your visit by remaining in France for as long as you wish, but as my guests?'

The offer was so unexpected that for a moment she could only stare at him. 'I . . . don't know. I shall have to speak to my father about it before giving you an answer.'

'Perhaps I should be the one to do that,' he decided firmly.

'Paul, are you sure we shan't be inconveniencing you?'

'*Ma petite,* I would not have made the offer if I had thought that.'

'It would be lovely,' she mused.

'But of course. It will mean that you can stay longer than you anticipated, and you will be able to see more of my country at your leisure while in the comfort of my home.'

'Yes.' And I shall see more of you as well, she thought to herself.

'Let us not discuss it further until I have spoken to your father,' he suggested, and Catherine was quite willing to leave it at that, knowing that her father would fall in with whatever she decided.

When they arrived at the Hotel Boulevard later that afternoon, they found Charles Anderson in his suite, writing letters. Paul wasted no time in repeating his offer of hospitality, and Charles, eyebrows raised, set aside his pen and listened attentively.

'My home is on the outskirts of Paris and it is much quieter there. I shall place my car at your disposal so that you may travel about as you please.'

'That is very kind of you, Dr. de Meillon, but we would not like to be a nuisance to you,' Charles protested.

'*Monsieur*, my sister and I are out of the house all day. It would only be during the evenings that we should all be together. I am sure that you would not find it such a strain to have me as your host for those few hours a day?'

'I wouldn't know about that,' Charles laughed, 'I only know that I certainly shan't find it a strain being your guest.'

'Well, then?'

'Catherine?' Charles cast a questioning glance in her direction and saw the answer written plainly on her face.

'It . . . would be very nice.' She turned to Paul. 'I think it's extremely kind of you to make this offer.'

It was with far more than kindness in his mind that Paul had made this suggestion. He needed more time to spend with Catherine. In his home she would be more accessible to him and their meetings would not have to be contrived.

'Dr. de Meillon, we accept your offer gladly,' Charles interrupted his thoughts, and Paul relaxed visibly for the first time.

They made arrangements that Paul would call for them the following afternoon as there were still a few business commitments Charles had to attend to, and then, raising Catherine's hand to his lips, Paul bade them *au revoir*.

If Catherine had wanted them to prolong their stay in Paris, Charles would not have objected, despite Paul's very generous offer. He had seen his daughter come alive in the Frenchman's company and realized, at last, the reason for her unhappiness so many months ago.

Should anything develop from their association, then their stay at Paul's home would also afford Charles the opportunity of becoming better acquainted with Paul de Meillon himself.

The hours dragged for Catherine until the time they had arranged that Paul would call for them. Charles had spent the best part of the day in town while Catherine packed their suitcases and settled their account. When Paul eventually arrived, she was nervous and edgy and hardly spoke at all as they drove through the city. Charles on the other hand was in a talkative mood, and thankfully she relaxed in her seat and allowed him to continue his conversation with Paul.

By the time they reached the Château de Bonheur, as Paul had said his home was called, she was more relaxed and could look about her with interest. The car slid through the wrought iron gates and up the driveway lined with chestnut trees. The house was impressive with its marble pillars at the entrance and the small balconies leading from several rooms on the upper floor. It was the type of house where one would expect to find a butler in attendance, but then this was France, and butlers were almost out of style.

As the car drew to a halt beside the steps, the massive front door opened and a young girl stepped out to welcome them.

'Come and meet our guests, Adèle,' Paul called. He made the introductions and from the moment Catherine's eyes met Adèle's, there was a feeling of mutual liking and respect. So this, at last, was Paul's sister. She was not at all like her brother. Although her hair was dark and so also her eyes, she had a heart-shaped face with fine features. There was absolutely no further resemblance to the lean hardness of Paul's outward appearance.

'Paul has told me so much about you that I have anxiously been awaiting your arrival,' she explained in her soft-spoken voice with its slightly foreign accent. 'Come, Paul, let us take their luggage and show them to their rooms.'

Encumbered with suitcases, they went indoors and up the stairs with its carved wooden balustrade, to the rooms which had been prepared for them.

'Paul will show you to your suite, Monsieur Anderson,' Adèle told Charles. 'Come, Catherine, your suite is this way.'

She turned to the left and then along a short passage, the thickly carpeted floor muffling their footsteps.

'This is your suite,' she announced, opening the door and placing the suitcase on the floor beside the bed. 'It is north-facing and overlooks the rose garden. In the summer it is ablaze with colour and you wake each morning with the scent of roses in your nostrils. Your bathroom is through this door,' she said, pointing towards the only other door leading from the room. 'You will be quite private here.'

She turned then to face Catherine, who stood open-mouthed taking in the magnificent draperies on the fourposter bed. The room was beautifully furnished and decidedly feminine with its lilac and white colour scheme. The curtains parted at the window after a gentle tug on the sash cord, and she exclaimed with delight as she noticed a small balcony beyond the second window. This was not merely a window, but a full length glass door leading on to her own private balcony.

'Do you like it?' Adèle asked directly behind her.

'Like it?' Catherine sighed ecstatically. '   a word strong enough to express how marvellous it is.' A sudden thought came to her. 'Did you choose this room for me, Adèle?'

'I did,' the girl admitted shyly.

Touched, Catherine took her hand and squeezed it. 'Thank you, Adèle, for your kindness.'

'Do not be too long, Adèle,' Paul called from further down the passage. 'Monsieur Anderson and I shall be waiting for you in the living-room.'

'We shall be down in a moment, *mon frère*,' she called back.

'Château de Bonheur,' Catherine mused. 'What does it mean?'

'Château of Happiness,' Adèle told her. 'I am told that my grandfather named it so when he brought my Grand'mère Adèle here as a bride.'

How poignant, Catherine thought, a lump rising to her throat.

'How many rooms are there in this house, Adèle?'

'About fifteen.'

'Do they all have a private bathroom?'

'Goodness, no,' Adèle laughed. 'These rooms are for special guests, and Paul said that you were special, so . . .'

'Do you often have people to stay?'

'Not often,' she admitted regretfully. 'Paul is not one for entertaining much.' She glanced at the suitcases. 'Would you like me to help you unpack?'

'I'll manage, thank you, Adèle. Perhaps we'd better go down and join the others.'

'*Oui*, but before we go,' Adèle stopped, looking slightly uncomfortable. 'Forgive me for asking this, but – is there something between you and Paul?'

Catherine hesitated. 'Why do you ask, Adèle?'

The girl shrugged. 'My brother has never yet invited a woman to his home. Not even one accompanied by her papa, as you are.'

'Your brother operated on me while he was in South Africa and we saw quite a bit of each other, but there is nothing else,' Catherine confessed, thankful that this at least was the truth. There *was* nothing between Paul and herself except friendship, despite the fact that she would have wished for more.

'We had better go down,' Adèle said at last. 'Paul does not like to be kept waiting.'

Catherine followed her along the short passage and down the stairs with the portraits of the de Meillon ancestors lining the walls. Adèle led the way into a warm, pleasantly furnished room where a fire burnt lustily in the grate. The room had a warmth which was not entirely due to the fire. It was a room that was lived in; a friendly room where one could relax and be oneself, shedding the problems of the day.

'So you have at last arrived,' Paul remarked.

'I'm sorry we kept you waiting, Paul,' Catherine apologized quickly.

'No matter. What will you have to drink, *chérie*?' he asked as they were seated. 'A Dubonnet, perhaps?'

'That would be lovely, thank you.'

'The usual Pernod for you, Adèle?'

'*Merci*, Paul.'

'After dinner I will show you through the house, Catherine,' Paul said, handing her her drink. 'My grandfather originally had this house built. It was my father's home, and now it is mine.' There was pride in his voice as he spoke. 'There are too many rooms which stand empty most of the time, but I would never consider selling the Château de Bonheur for something smaller.'

'I don't blame you, Dr. de Meillon,' Charles agreed. 'You have a truly beautiful home.'

'I thank you, *monsieur*,' Paul bowed slightly before seating himself, 'but please do call me Paul.'

'Paul it is. Tell me, that painting on the wall, is it . . .?'

'It is a painting of Maman,' Adèle told Charles quickly. 'It was painted by a crippled artist who sought shelter here during the war. It is very good, is it not?'

'Very lifelike, yes,' he admitted. 'You are very like your mother, my dear.'

'*Merci, monsieur*, it is kind of you to say so,' Adèle smiled with pleasure. 'I did not know Maman at all. She died not long after I was born. In my life there has only been Papa and Paul, and now . . . there is only Paul.'

Catherine noticed the slight hesitation and was suddenly curious to know more about Adèle.

'Paul tells me you're doing well with your boutique,' Charles changed the subject.

'Oh, yes.'

Charles Anderson had a way with people and nearly always succeeded in getting them to talk about themselves. He plied Adèle with questions which she answered eagerly, delighted that he should show such an interest.

Catherine's glance met Paul's across the room and her heart fluttered oddly. She would really have to exercise greater control over her emotions in future, she decided. He looked very much at ease as he sat in the leather armchair beside the fire sipping his drink. Yet, despite the look of outward calm, Catherine sensed the aura of restlessness about him.

Their glances met once more, and this time he smiled and raised his glass in silent salute. Catherine's lips curved into an answering smile as she returned the toast, and then, conscious of the fact that he was still looking at her, she blushed and endeavoured to concentrate on the conversation between her father and Adèle.

Paul, twirling the amber liquid in his glass, knew a feeling of impatience. How right she looked, sitting there close to the fire with the light playing in her coppery hair. Her hands, cradling the glass in her lap, were small and slender, the nails tinted a delicate pink. How soft they had been on the occasions he had raised them to his lips! He recalled the gentle fragrance of her perfume when, at times, she had been close to him. So fresh; so appealing; and so delightful to the senses.

He literally shook himself out of his reverie, drained his glass, and got to his feet.

'Come, it is time we had dinner,' he announced, placing Catherine's hand on his arm, and leading the way.

Despite the fact that they lived under the same roof, Catherine hardly ever saw Paul alone. During the day she and her father drove into the country in a hired car – Charles had refused Paul's offer of the use of Paul's own car – and explored France at their leisure. The evenings they spent together, either discussing what they had seen or asking Paul's advice about their intended trip the following day.

It was not until two weeks after their arrival at the Château de Bonheur that Paul and Catherine had a few moments alone. Charles retired to bed soon after dinner, and Adèle rushed off to her seamstress with several new designs for the spring fashion show she was planning.

Paul placed a record on the turntable and for a while they sat in silence as the pleasant strains of Dvorak's 'Humoresque' filled the air. It was relaxing just to lie there in the armchair, listening appreciatively to the music, yet every fibre of her being was acutely conscious of his presence. It was alarming the effect this man had on her. The desire to escape and the desire to stay were equally strong, as Catherine remained seated, caught between two conflicting emotions like a bird caught helplessly in a trap.

'You are very quiet, *chérie*?' Paul remarked as the music ended. 'Do you not care for my choice of record?'

'Oh, no! I enjoyed it tremendously,' she contradicted, and then, for want of anything better to say, she asked: 'Do you like the classics?'

He shrugged and lit the inevitable cigarette, stretching his long legs out in front of him towards the fire burning in the grate. 'It depends entirely on my frame of mind. I must also confess, *chérie*, that I do not care much for this modern stuff they call music.'

Catherine laughed. 'I can't entirely blame you. Some of it is quite atrocious.'

Is this *me* talking? she wondered. The girl who used to love all the latest pop songs and never missed a party. In fact, the wilder the party was, the better?

'You are frowning, *ma chérie*,' Paul said quietly. 'You were thinking of something nasty, perhaps?'

'No.' Catherine hesitated. It would be impossible to explain to Paul the change he had unwittingly brought about in her.

'Have you seen all you have wanted to of my country during the past two weeks?' he asked, flicking his cigarette ash carefully into the ashtray.

'I have seen quite a lot, Paul, and I am only sorry that I shan't be able to see the South of France as well.'

'Why not?' he asked, suddenly alert. 'You are not thinking of going back to South Africa yet, are you?'

'I am, Paul,' she admitted, watching the flames casting weird patterns on the opposite wall. 'We're thinking of leaving within the next few days. So you see, the South of France will just have to remain unexplored by the Andersons.' She smiled slightly, trying to hide the acute sadness in her heart.

'Perhaps you might yet see the Côte d'Azur, *chérie*. Who knows?'

'Who knows?' she echoed sadly, fingering the crocheted lace at her fingertips.

There was a moment of silence as they each sat deep in thought, and it was Paul who finally shattered it.

'I am leaving for Grasse early in the morning. There is a patient there a colleague of mine would like me to see.' He sat forward in his chair and there was an urgency in his voice which Catherine had not heard before. 'I shall be away for no more than three days. Promise me, *chérie*, that you will not leave until I have returned. Promise me this, *ma très chère*.'

There it was again. *Ma très chère*. What did it mean? Perhaps Adèle would tell her if she asked.

'Well?' Paul asked impatiently.

'I promise, Paul. We won't leave until you have returned home.'

Charles Anderson agreed readily to Catherine's suggestion that they postpone their departure until Paul had returned from his visit to Grasse. Once again the time to part drew near, and Catherine knew she would not be able to still the pain in her heart as she had done once before.

During Paul's absence Catherine missed him dreadfully. She tried pretending to herself that he was at the Clinic and would be returning home as soon as evening drew near, but this façade only lasted until after dinner, then reality stepped in and she was left despondent.

On the second evening after Paul's departure, Catherine went for a stroll in the garden. It was a matter of hours now before he would return, and she was like a child on the eve of a party. The icy breeze whipped against her face and left her feeling exhilarated. For the first time she thought of David Marsden waiting for her to return to Cape Town. She had sent him a few postcards but had not managed to sit down to write a long letter. Her news could perhaps wait until she had returned to South Africa, she decided.

David loved her and wanted to marry her, but ... her thoughts drifted back to Paul. It was going to be so much more difficult saying good-bye for the second time, and even more impossible to forget. How naïve she had been to think that it had all been imagination, when merely hearing his voice had revived the love she had carried hidden in her heart. This love, though futile, was for ever. For ever! the breeze sighed as, blinking away the tears, she retraced her steps to the house.

On the patio she paused briefly to stare longingly down the driveway. Oh, if only it were tomorrow when she would see his car come sweeping up the drive, she thought impatiently.

With a sigh she turned, only to stand frozen the next instant. There before her stood Paul, his arms outstretched, a smile on his lips. Without a second thought she rushed towards him and buried her face against his shoulder as his arm closed about her protectively.

'Paul! Paul!' she cried, her voice muffled against the expensive softness of his jacket. 'When did you come? Why didn't I hear you?'

'I came only a few minutes ago,' Paul laughed, holding her slightly away from him. 'I left my car in the lane outside and walked up the driveway. That is why you did not hear me. Was it a nice surprise, *chérie*?'

'Oh, Paul, yes!' she laughed happily. 'We weren't expecting you until tomorrow morning.'

'I managed to get away sooner, and so ... here I am.'

Catherine extricated herself self-consciously from his arms and cursed herself for the spontaneity of her greeting. What must Paul be thinking of her?

'Come,' he said brusquely, taking her arm. 'Let us go through to my study. I have brought you a small gift and I am anxious to know whether it will be to your liking.'

'Oh, Paul, no!' she cried, abashed, but he waved aside her protestations as they entered the house.

She had only been in Paul's study once before and that was on the evening they had arrived. She was once again struck by the masculinity of the furniture and impressed by the rows of books which lined the walls. He was obviously fond of poetry, for there were books of Keats and Milton which had immediately caught her eye.

From his medical bag he produced a small parcel, carefully wrapped and tied with a ribbon. 'This is for you, *chérie*.'

For a moment she held it without opening it. Then, sensing Paul's growing agitation, she ripped off the wrapping until she held in her hand a small phial of perfume. Removing the top, she inhaled the delicate, tantalizing fragrance. It was subtle and expensive.

'Paul,' she breathed, 'you shouldn't have done this, but it was wonderful of you to think of me in this way.'

'Grasse is noted for its perfumes,' he explained. And then, rather hesitantly, 'You like it?'

'Like it? Oh, Paul, I simply love it!' A flicker of sadness crossed her sensitive face. 'I shall think of you and remember your kindness each time I use this gift. Thank you very much, Paul.'

'You are leaving soon?' he asked, looking at her intently.

'Yes.' She placed the phial on the desk and walked across to the window. 'We're booked on a flight to London the day after tomorrow.'

The chestnut trees on either side of the driveway stood like dark giants swaying in the gentle breeze. The peaceful serenity of Paul's home, and the magnificence of the gardens, was something she would remember for ever. The lights of Paris were flickering in the distance, and Catherine was certain that one could not visit this great pulsating city, without being filled with sweet nostalgia.

She could no longer enjoy the view as Paul's hands closed about her waist. Excitement pulsed through her veins and quickened her heartbeats.

'*Mon coeur*,' he whispered in an anguished voice. 'I cannot let you go!'

She turned in his arms, wide-eyed and pleading. The next instant she was crushed against his lean hardness, as his lips came down and claimed her own in a kiss that drew the very soul from within her breast.

Again and again he kissed her, whispering endearments in his own language which, although she could not understand, conveyed to her the extent of his passion. Never for a moment, even in her wildest fancies, had she imagined this wild pulsating desire which coursed through her being as he caressed her possessively, almost as if he wanted to imprint every part of her on his memory.

With her arms wound tightly about his neck, she submitted to his lovemaking; indeed she revelled in it, returning his kisses until passion flared and sanity almost deserted them.

Suddenly she was freed, and she tottered against the wall at the unexpectedness of it.

'Forgive me, *chérie*,' Paul apologized hoarsely. 'Forgive me! I had no right to do that. No right at all. *Mon dieu!*' He passed a hand across his face as he turned away from her, but not before Catherine had seen the agonized expression in his eyes and a certain grimness about the mouth which she had kissed so passionately only a moment ago.

Dazed for a while, she could not react, and then she flung herself across the space which separated them and clutched his arm, forcing him to face her.

'Paul! What is the matter?' she cried anxiously, almost shaking him. 'How can you say that you shouldn't have kissed me like that?'

'Because I should not have, *chérie*,' he persisted doggedly, with a calmness that almost infuriated her.

Frantic now to get to the bottom of his strange behaviour, she threw her pride out the window, not stopping to choose her words carefully.

'If you're asking me to believe that you go about kissing women just for fun of it, only to regret it a moment later,' she cried, close to tears, 'then you'll have to do better than that.'

'Catherine, you are overwrought and upset,' he said quietly. 'What is a kiss, after all?'

'That wasn't *just* a kiss!' she flared, and Paul stared fascinated at the anger in her glittering, green eyes. 'You kissed me as though . . . as though you cared, and surely you realized in the way I . . . I returned your kisses that I . . .'

'*Chérie*,' Paul interrupted, equally determined to make an end to this subject, 'you are young and impressionable. If any other man had kissed you in the same way as I did a few moments ago, you would have reacted in the same way.'

'Nonsense!' The tears were brimming in her eyes as she made an effort to gather her scattered wits about her. She was fighting now for her very existence. 'Don't be so sceptical, Paul. Don't be so wary to accept the love I have to offer you. Yes, I love you,' she repeated as she saw his heavy eyebrows lift above his eyes. 'No doubt you think I'm being absolutely brazen, and perhaps I am. Time is running out, so let's be truthful just this once, Paul.'

The light of battle in her eyes enchanted him, but he steeled himself against it. Their association had been too brief. How could he be sure of her? They needed more time, he resolved. Perhaps he should follow them to South Africa after all. There, at least, he would not have to divide his time between the Clinic and her.

'You don't love me, Catherine,' he said eventually, his voice cold and clipped with the effort to keep his emotions in check. 'What you feel for me is gratitude. You are grateful for what I did for you. I sensed this in your attitude towards me after your operation in Cape Town, and although I appreciate it, I want more from a wife than just gratitude.'

Catherine winced as he spoke and knew her task to

95

be almost impossible. There was one question, however, she was forced to ask.

'Do you love me, Paul?'

'*Bon dieu!*' he gestured angrily. 'You have no right to ask me that.'

'I think I have, dearest Paul,' she insisted quietly with pounding heart. 'If your answer is "no", then we shall not speak about this subject again and I shall return to my own country within two days, and we shall never see each other again.'

Paul stared at her for a moment. In her eyes there shone a light of sincerity, and . . . was it love? Was he being purposely blind to what was there for all the world to see? Were his fears completely unfounded? Soon she would depart from his life and he would perhaps never see her again. Would he, he wondered desperately, be able to endure the finality of this parting?

His expression remained unrelenting, and Catherine turned away. She had fought and lost, and her aching heart was of little comfort. As she reached the door, she suddenly found her exit barred.

'Do you really love me, *chérie?*'

'Yes.' Her heart leapt.

'This is not just gratitude?'

'No, no! A thousand times, no!'

'*Adorée!*' Miraculously she was in his arms once more, and his lips parted hers in the passion of his kiss. '*Je suis fou de toi!* I am mad about you,' he translated.

'Paul?' she asked several minutes later. 'What does *ma très chère* mean?'

He laughed softly and kissed her swiftly before answering. 'It means "my very dear".'

'When did you first know that you loved me?' the

inevitable question was asked.

'From the first moment I looked into your eyes. They fascinated me.'

'I can't believe that you really love me,' she sighed with wonder.

From the inner breast pocket of his jacket he produced a scarf which she recognized instantly as the one he had asked to keep as a memento. 'Would I carry this with me if I did not love you?'

'Oh, Paul!' she breathed tremulously as she watched him pocket the scarf before taking her into his arms once more.

'And you, *mignonne*? When did you know?' he asked, sliding his lips along her cheek.

'I think I knew for certain that evening you came into my ward and found Ronnie Jansen molesting me,' she admitted, burying her face against his neck. 'Why have we wasted so much time, my darling?'

'We are not wasting any more time than we have to, *mon coeur*,' he said firmly. 'This very minute I am going to ask your father's permission to marry you as soon as possible.' He looked down at her seriously as she lay in his arms, and pushed his fingers through her coppery curls until his hand rested in the nape of her neck. 'It would matter very much to you if you are not married in your own country?'

'Darling Paul!' she cried, encircling his waist with her arms. 'I don't very much care where we're married, as long as we can be together now, and for always.'

Prophetic words, perhaps foolishly spoken, for the future is always a mystery which unfolds day by day.

CHAPTER SIX

CHARLES ANDERSON once again postponed his departure in view of his daughter's forthcoming marriage. It did not come at all as a surprise to him, for he had suspected for quite some time that Paul de Meillon had won his daughter's heart. The few weeks they had spent at the Château de Bonheur had given Charles the opportunity of becoming better acquainted with his future son-in-law, and what he had seen, he had liked very much.

Catherine and Paul were married quietly a few days later with Charles, Adèle, and a colleague of Paul's, John Dunbury, and his wife Susan present as guests. The sun pushed through the clouds like a silent blessing as they left the church and drove to Paul's home, where the staff had prepared an excellent meal to match this joyous occasion. Adèle had been thrilled that she was able to supply Catherine with a wedding gown from her boutique at such short notice, and she was even more delighted at the prospect of acquiring a sister-in-law, of whom she approved wholeheartedly.

It was with mixed emotions that Catherine bade her father farewell at the airport later that day. Although tearful at her father's departure, she was as yet overawed by the wondrous realization that she was Paul de Meillon's wife, and quite unused to the heavy feeling of the glittering gold band on her third finger left hand. It was unbelievable that it was only a few days ago that Paul had asked her to marry him. The speed with which it had all been arranged had left neither of them with time to have last-minute doubts.

When Charles Anderson's plane finally disappeared amongst the clouds, they left the airport and drove south for a short honeymoon at the coast. They were married at last, and now there would be no more partings in the future, Catherine thought, as she sat admiring her wedding ring and marvelling at the happiness which flowed through her.

Several kilometres out of Paris, Paul stopped the car and removed his jacket and tie. When he slid behind the wheel once more, he took her in his arms and they exchanged a long and satisfying kiss.

'We are alone at last,' he sighed, looking down at Catherine. 'These past few days have been exhausting for us both, *mon coeur*. Now we can begin to relax and enjoy ourselves.'

'Wonderful thought!' she breathed ecstatically, smiling up at him.

'You have no regrets, *mignonne*?'

'Not unless you turn out to be a bully and a tyrant,' she teased, a hint of laughter in her eyes.

'I shall whip you every day,' Paul threatened with mock severity, 'and if you do not listen to me I shall chain you to the wall of the dungeon at the Château de Bonheur. So beware!'

'You frighten me to death!' she gasped playfully. 'I shall walk in fear of you for the rest of my days.'

'And so you should.'

How delightful it was to be just a little foolish. To tease and be teased; to love and be loved. This was a Paul she had yet to become fully acquainted with, and the prospect was exhilarating.

'I love you, Catherine,' Paul groaned, sliding his lips along her cheek towards her ear, 'but if I do not let you go now and start driving, I will be making love to you right here, and our arrival in Cannes will most certainly be delayed.'

He laughed softly as Catherine blushed becomingly, and planted a kiss on the tip of her nose before starting the car to continue their journey.

The Côte d'Azur was all that Paul had said it would be, and more – warm, fragrant and vivid with colour, like a picture out of a travel brochure. Paul's villa was perched on a hill overlooking a narrow strip of beach, where they bathed daily in the azure sea and dried themselves on the golden sand.

'One cannot be in Cannes and not visit one of the casinos,' Paul announced one evening, and so Catherine was allowed a glimpse of the places where gambling for high stakes was an everyday occurrence. Paul stood by tolerantly while she tried her hand at the roulette table and was lucky enough to double her money.

'Beginner's luck,' she had laughed excitedly as one of the casino staff encouraged her to continue.

'But you will be lucky again,' the swarthy gent insisted, taking her arm. 'A lady as beautiful as yourself cannot lose.'

At that moment Paul stepped in. 'I think my wife has had enough, *monsieur*,' he said with icy politeness, placing an arm about her shoulders.

Catherine glanced up at him thankfully as the man shrugged slightly and strolled away.

'Perhaps we have seen enough for one night, *mon amour*?' Paul asked, a smile playing about his lips. 'You have proved your prowess at roulette, and also that you have a fatal charm for the opposite sex.'

'Paul, don't be silly,' Catherine spoke above the noise in the casino. 'It wasn't I who charmed him but the money I had won.'

'We will not argue, *ma petite*,' Paul teased as he

placed her wrap about her shoulders. 'I think it is time I took my wife home before she is snatched from under my very nose.'

'Paul de Meillon, you are a fool, and a darling.'

'When we reach the villa,' Paul said, helping her into the car, 'you shall repeat those words. And make sure that the light of love is in your eyes, for I do not like being called a fool and a darling in the same breath.'

'Do you intend whipping me, dear husband?' she asked, joining in with Paul's teasing mood.

'That depends entirely on you, my love,' he threatened smilingly.

When they arrived at the villa she duly repeated her statement, only to be swept into his arms and carried laughingly up the stairs and into their bedroom, where their laughter turned to whispers of passion.

They remained on the Côte d'Azur long enough to attend the carnival in Nice which, as Paul patiently told her, takes place every year during February. Although he had told her a little about this custom, Catherine had not expected such an elaborate affair. There were gorgeous floral displays and fireworks which took her breath away. The music, the parade of floats with their grotesque figures made from papier-mâché, was to her quite enthralling.

Paul, who had seen it all before, observed instead her reactions with much amusement, and teased her about her childlike enthusiasm.

'You are like a child out on her first Sunday School picnic,' he laughed, tugging at her coppery curls.

'I'm sorry, Paul, if you've found it all boring,' she apologized, 'but to me it's all been quite enchanting and exciting.'

The excitement mounted amongst the crowds as the

next parade of floats passed by, and Catherine discovered that she was being pushed away from Paul.

'Here,' he said, gripping her hand tightly, 'you had better hang on to me, *chérie*, or we will be separated. In this crowd it will be almost impossible to find each other again.'

They fought their way towards a small café and in the shade of a tarpaulin Paul ordered them each a long, cool drink, which they sipped while watching the parade in comfort.

'You have enjoyed yourself, *mon coeur*?' Paul asked, his manner more serious. 'You have not yet regretted marrying me and allowing your father to return to your country alone?'

Catherine clasped his hands across the table, the laughter in her eyes replaced by a look of sincerity. 'I haven't regretted it for one moment, my darling. I love you, Paul, more than I ever thought possible.'

No man can withstand such an ardent declaration and Paul was only human. With his free hand he pulled her head closer and kissed her pink lips quickly, and passionately.

'Drink up, my love, there is much I still want to show you. It is a perfect day, and we shall take a leisurely route back to the villa so that you can see the Mediterranean coast at its best.'

It was indeed a leisurely trip as Paul had suggested. They stopped often to enable her to drink in the beauty of the scene surrounding her. To her left was the sea, with the shimmering intensity of the sunlight on the vivid blue. To her right, the deep velvety green of the foliage. Eucalyptus and orange trees, her sense of smell informed her. The mimosa in flower on the hillside was like a bride's bouquet, and straight ahead of her the red rocks of the Estérel coast against the cloudless sky.

'Oh, Paul,' she sighed, 'this is truly beautiful.' She turned to him then. 'Will we come again one day?'

'My villa is always there at our disposal,' he reminded her, 'and my staff are always prepared for my unexpected arrival.'

'You are finding my country very beautiful, Catherine,' Paul said that evening as they sat on the patio watching the moon turn the sea to silver. 'Do not forget that your own country was to me just as beautiful.'

'There is an old-world beauty about Europe which fascinates me,' she admitted, fingering the sprig of mimosa Paul had picked for her on the way back to the villa. 'It's totally different from the rugged beauty of my own country, and it can't be compared. You become accustomed to what you see, and perhaps slightly bored when others show enthusiasm for something which is to you just part of your life. It's only when you see it again through the eyes of a stranger that you notice the majestic mountains, the green valleys with their vineyards and old homesteads. Even the flat land of my country has a beauty all its own.'

Her eyes were dreamy as she spoke, and Paul felt a twinge of regret for uprooting her from the country she loved, and transplanting her in the unknown environment of his own country.

'I shall never stand in your way if you should wish to pay your father a visit,' he offered. 'You need only to say when you wish to go and I shall arrange everything for you.'

She looked at him suddenly and smiled tenderly. 'My place is with you, Paul, and I have no intention of hopping back and forth between South Africa and France at the merest whim.'

'*Adorée!*' he breathed, pulling her out of her chair

and into his arms. 'I do not deserve a love such as yours.'

Catherine raised her lips to his and welcomed the languid feeling that stole through her whenever he held her as he did then. His hands caressed her, moving her to a passion which she found awe inspiring.

'Paul,' she moaned softly, swaying against him, 'I love you so.'

With a muttered exclamation he lifted her and carried her into the intimate darkness of the villa, his footsteps silent on the carpeted floor.

On the now deserted patio, a sprig of mimosa lay forgotten. In the morning the maid would sweep it away as these two weeks had been swept aside to become a lingering memory of the happy, carefree days they had spent together.

'You are very silent, Catherine,' Paul remarked as they travelled into the hills near Grasse the following day. The air for miles around was perfumed with the scent of lilies, carnations and mimosa. 'Are you not happy to be returning to Paris with me?'

He had noticed her almost brooding silence soon after they had left Cannes, and it troubled him. Sensitive to her every mood, and caught in the web of his own fears, he remained silent as well, until the agony of it forced him to speak.

'You do not answer me,' he persisted as she turned to face him, a hesitant smile on her lips.

'I can't rid myself of the ridiculous feeling that our happiness is like a delicate soap bubble which could burst at any moment,' she replied, frowning once more.

Paul stopped the car on a hill from where they could overlook the valley. He, too, was serious as he faced her.

'Are you regretting our marriage?'

Catherine shivered involuntarily. Paul had asked this question constantly during the two weeks they had been married. Could his uncertainty as to her feelings for him be the cause of this morbid fear which persisted in dogging her happiest moments? she wondered.

The fear in her heart was clearly visible in her expressive eyes as she placed a hand on either side of his face, and met his glance steadily.

'Paul, my darling, I love you. Whatever happens, please don't ever doubt that.'

He heard the urgency in her voice, and felt it in her hands. What a fool he was to doubt her love; her sincerity. Had she not proved to him during these two blissful weeks at the coast that she was his and his alone?

For the next few minutes they were oblivious of their picturesque surroundings as, locked in each other's arms, they vowed their love anew.

Adèle welcomed them home effusively, and even Greta, Paul's housekeeper, left the sanctuary of her kitchen to say how pleased she was that Monsieur le Docteur and Madame were home at last.

The Château de Bonheur had undergone a minor change in their absence. On Paul's instructions, the master bedroom, which had not been occupied for so many years, was re-opened and stylishly redecorated in a delicate rose-pink.

The magnificently carved fourposter bed, with its white lace canopy and flowing drapes, had been in the de Meillon family for generations, Paul told her. Catherine admired the splendid craftsmanship and took a great delight in inspecting her new domain.

A smaller room adjoined the master bedroom and

could be used as a dressing-room. There was also a single divan in the room with a chest of drawers, a full-length mirror, and a comfortable chair.

'You are satisfied, *mon coeur*?' Paul asked eventually, a smile hovering about his lips.

Catherine spread her arms wide with wonder. 'You had all this done for me?'

'But of course.'

'Paul!' she cried, flinging her arms about his neck and kissing him spontaneously. 'It's absolutely beautiful, and I love you for it.'

Adèle stood to one side watching this display of affection with a wistful expression on her young face, but her brother and his wife were too occupied with each other to notice.

To ward off the loneliness Catherine spent most of her days pottering in the garden, or indoors, supervising the evening meal. But even this was unnecessary, for Greta was excellently trained and so also the rest of the staff.

A letter arrived from her father. He had had a pleasant trip back to South Africa and was missing her. He consoled himself with the idea that she was in Paul's capable hands, and knew that she would be well taken care of. There was a postscript from Sarah in which she wished them every happiness and hoped they would be blessed with many children.

Catherine laughed happily at this. It was so typical of the coloured people. There just had to be a family to bind the union, and bring the ultimate happiness.

There was also a letter from David Marsden, addressed to them both.

'My dear friends,' he had written, 'It came as no surprise to hear of your marriage. I have always known that your heart belonged to Paul, Cathy, but I foolishly hoped that this could be overcome. Perhaps I should never have let you go on that overseas trip, for I knew on the day we parted that I had lost.

'Paul, my friend, the best man has won. I wish you both the very best in life. Look after Cathy, for she is very dear to me, or you shall have David Marsden to contend with.'

This amused Paul as he read it, for David was a whole head shorter than Paul, and slenderly built, whereas Paul was broad-shouldered, tall, and physically the more superior of the two.

'I hope we shall meet again in the future,' David concluded, 'either on one of my rare visits to Europe, or on one of your visits to South Africa. Regards, David.'

Paul dropped the letter into Catherine's lap and placed an arm about her shoulders as they sat at the fireside before retiring for the evening.

'We shall return often to your country, *mon coeur*,' he promised. 'I do not wish to alienate you from your father, and there is still much to explore of your country.'

Catherine smiled happily and snuggled her head on to his shoulder.

'It is time my colleagues were introduced to my lovely wife,' Paul remarked. 'I shall invite a few over on Friday evening for dinner, if you think you have settled down well enough to cope?'

'Of course I shall be able to cope,' she assured him quickly, in spite of the anxious feeling that settled at the pit of her stomach. 'How many do you intend inviting?'

'I think I shall ask the Dunburys, whom you met at our wedding, and the Chiltons. Both couples are from England, so there will be no lapsing into French to make it difficult for you to follow the conversation.' Paul was thoughtful for a moment. 'Perhaps I shall invite Félix le Clergé as well. He is our pathologist and would at least make the number even.'

Catherine swallowed the lump in her throat and assured him once again that it would be in order. After all, where she failed Greta, who was an excellent cook, would cope admirably.

The evening of the dinner party arrived all too soon. Catherine was nervous about the whole affair. It would be the first time she would be hostess to Paul's colleagues and friends, and everything had to be absolutely perfect. Adèle, to whom the success of this occasion was of no importance, laughed away Catherine's nervousness and helped immensely where she could.

Greta, who was originally from Germany, had been employed as cook at the Château de Bonheur when Adèle was but a child. During this time Paul had relied entirely on her when he had been forced to entertain guests, and never once had he been disappointed.

'Madame need not trouble herself,' she had told Catherine that morning. 'Everything shall be done to Madame's wishes.'

'I'm sorry, Greta,' Catherine apologized sincerely. 'I don't doubt your capabilities for one moment.'

'I understand,' she smiled. 'Madame is nervous.'

Satisfied, Catherine had left Greta to continue with her preparations.

Paul had disliked the idea of a buffet supper, so the main dining hall with the long, impressive table, had been prepared for the guests.

'Are you certain I haven't forgotten anything, Adèle?' Catherine asked agitatedly as she flicked her eyes over the decoratively laid table, with its damask tablecloth and gleaming silver.

'Of course not!' Adèle assured her. 'Everything is going to be *magnifique*! Do not worry so.'

'But the dinner?'

'*Chérie*, you gave your instructions to Greta, did you not?'

'Yes, I did, but—'

'Then do stop worrying about everything,' Adèle insisted, placing an arm about Catherine's shoulders and giving her a reassuring hug. 'Come. Soon Paul will be home and we have not even started dressing yet.' She glanced at Catherine curiously as they made their way upstairs. 'What are you wearing, Cathy?'

'I thought the blue dress,' Catherine replied, uncertainty creeping into her voice again. 'It's soft, just the right length, and not too elaborate.'

Adèle considered this for a moment. '*Oui*, you are right. It accentuates your slimness and gives you an almost . . . ethereal look.'

'Good heavens!' Catherine exclaimed laughingly. 'I don't think I very much like the idea of looking ethereal.'

'Angelic, then,' Adèle supplemented with a grin. 'You will look angelic, and everyone will just love you.'

'Oh, dear, Paul won't care for *that* very much!' Catherine laughed dubiously as they parted.

Paul arrived some time later while Catherine was still doing her hair. He stood regarding her for a moment, with his hand still resting on the doorknob. Meeting his glance, Catherine felt her pulse rate quicken as his eyes slid over her sparsely clad figure.

She had not yet become accustomed to the look of ardour in his eyes. The happiness they shared was still too new; too unbelievable to grasp fully. And so also her moments of extreme happiness were clouded with an intense fear that at any moment it could slip from her grasp to be lost for ever.

Paul had laughed at her when she had voiced her fears one evening as she lay in his arms, her head pillowed on his shoulder. But although she had tried to push these doubts aside, she found them returning relentlessly.

Now, as Paul dropped his hand to his side and came towards her, she felt again the aching fear course through her. Would they always feel this way about each other? Would her love be strong enough to convince him that he had not made an error in marrying her?

He pulled her up into his arms and Catherine pushed all other thoughts from her mind as she surrendered herself to his warm embrace and the passion his lips evoked within her.

'Our guests will be arriving soon,' she gasped as she eventually tore her lips from his.

'Ah, yes, our guests,' he sighed, releasing her.

'You are not nervous, are you?' he asked some time later when, bathed and shaven, he stood knotting his tie while she inspected her make-up in the mirror.

'A little,' she admitted readily. 'But then I always am when meeting strangers.'

'There is no need,' he assured her. 'The Dunburys are quite ordinary people, as you know, and so are the Chiltons. Félix de Clergé is a little ... well, we shall discuss that later.'

'Now you've made me inquisitive,' Catherine pouted playfully, but Paul remained deliberately obtuse as he placed a finger beneath her chin and kissed her hastily on the lips.

'It is time we went downstairs to await the arrival of our guests,' he smiled tantalizingly as he opened the door and stood aside for her to precede him.

Meeting Paul's colleagues was not such an ordeal as what Catherine had imagined, and after they had partaken of a light sherry, the dinner was served.

As the meal progressed, Catherine began to feel more at ease. She had been unnecessarily concerned, she realized, as she noticed the delight with which each dish was received. As on the occasion of their wedding, she found Dr. John Dunbury pleasant in a quiet sort of way, while his wife, Susan, had a shy sincerity about her which appealed to Catherine instantly. On the other hand, the Chiltons were talkative and inquisitive. Eileen Chilton, seated at Catherine's right, kept the conversation flowing constantly, her witty remarks reducing them all to laughter. In spite of the woman's outward appearance and general behaviour, a warning bell sounded somewhere at the back of Catherine's mind. She would have to take care where Eileen Chilton was concerned.

Adèle, seated opposite Félix le Clergé, appeared to be having difficulty in concentrating on her food. Her glances swept constantly towards Félix, and he too, was rather quiet as he continually glanced at Adèle from beneath his dark eyebrows, and smiled secretively.

If there was an understanding between the two, Catherine decided, then Paul, seated at the head of the table, was sublimely oblivious of the fact. Surely, if this was so, Adèle would have revealed something when she discovered that Félix would be amongst the invited guests? Catherine wondered, perplexed. Or had she been so engrossed in her own happiness that she had been blind to all else?

Eileen Chilton drew Catherine into the conversation at that moment, and for a while she forgot Adèle and Félix, and their peculiar behaviour.

'You must be lonely here in this vast house while Paul is at the clinic,' Eileen remarked. 'Have you made many friends?'

Catherine sensed that Paul was listening with divided attention to something John Dunbury was saying, and that he was all at once intensely interested in the trend of her conversation with Eileen Chilton.

'I'm not particularly lonely,' Catherine replied carefully, dabbing at her lips with her table-napkin. 'I spend a lot of time in the garden, and I do a lot of reading.'

'Do you go out much?'

'I occasionally go into town when I need something.'

Eileen Chilton gestured prettily with her bejewelled hand. 'You *must* come over to our place one day,' she offered.

'Thank you very much,' Catherine replied, making a silent resolution that this was one invitation she had no intention of accepting.

'I believe you are a South African?' Susan Dunbury joined in the conversation for the first time.

'Yes, I am,' Catherine acknowledged readily.

'My brother is a civil engineer in Johannesburg,' Susan continued. 'I don't suppose—'

'Catherine comes from Cape Town,' her husband interrupted gently. 'I am sure she wouldn't know many people in Johannesburg.'

'Cape Town?' Eileen exclaimed in surprise. 'Did you meet each other in Cape Town?'

Catherine glanced at Paul and noticed the all too familiar tightness about his mouth. He was displeased with the direction the conversation was heading, she knew instinctively.

'Yes, we met each other in Cape Town,' she admitted, a flicker of fear going through her.

'I wasn't aware that you had lectured in Cape Town as well, Paul?' Eileen persisted, glancing down the length of the table at him.

'You are quite correct,' Paul remarked, a tight smile about his lips. 'I did not lecture in Cape Town. However, I flew down to visit an old friend of mine who introduced me to Catherine.' He dropped his table-napkin on to the table and stood up. 'Shall we return to the living-room and have our coffee there?'

Everyone agreed to this suggestion and the conversation was instantly sent in a different direction.

Why had Paul been so agitated? Catherine wondered as she poured coffee from the silver coffee jug moments later. Why was he loath to mention the fact that she had once been his patient? Had she not yet convinced him sufficiently of the depth of her feelings to enable him to discuss that subject openly with others?

Susan, seated beside Catherine on the couch, whispered an apology.

'I always seem to say the wrong things at the wrong time,' she continued ruefully.

Catherine smiled at her reassuringly. This slender, dark-haired woman with the delicate Dresden features and gentle nature would be an asset to have as a friend, rather than the bombastic-natured Eileen Chilton, who at that moment was laughing loudly at her own joke.

'You've said nothing that needs an apology,' Catherine assured Susan Dunbury. 'There's nothing secretive about the way Paul and I met each other.

Perhaps I'll tell you one day, then you can judge for yourself.'

Satisfied, Susan relaxed while she sipped her coffee and relapsed into silence once more.

The rest of the evening passed pleasantly for Catherine. At one stage Félix approached her and offered to refill her glass, but when she refused, he remained for a moment longer to inquire whether life in France contrasted drastically with that of her own country.

'Not at all,' she hastened to assure him.

'Paris comes alive at night for the tourist.'

'Perhaps,' she smiled, 'but in my country the tourist need not wait for darkness to enjoy the pleasures it has to offer.'

'You are a staunch South African?' he asked with a mischievous smile.

'It is the country of my birth, Monsieur le Clergé. It is only natural, surely?'

'My remark was not meant as an insult, *madame*. Forgive me,' he bowed slightly.

Catherine laughed then. 'You needn't apologize, *monsieur*. I would love to tell you more about my country some day.'

Félix le Clergé had a certain charm about him which appealed to her. But then, she was sure, most women found him charming, especially when he spoke English with that heavy French accent. He plied her with questions about herself which she answered readily enough until several heads had turned in their direction. Félix, noticing this, finally returned to his chair, and sat staring morosely at the carpet for a time, while Catherine was left wondering why everyone had taken such an interest in the fact that Félix had chosen to spend a few minutes talking exclusively to her.

Shrugging off the feeling of irritation, Catherine

turned to Susan Dunbury and endeavoured to forget the many questions which plagued her mind.

The Dunburys were the first to leave that evening, then the Chiltons and Félix le Clergé. Adèle helped to disperse with the empty glasses and dirty ash-trays before beating a hasty retreat to her bedroom. When Catherine finally returned to the living-room, she found Paul smoking a last cigarette before going to bed.

He looked unusually pensive as he stood there staring into the dying embers of the fire. The events of the evening immediately crowded Catherine's mind once more. Although she longed to ask the questions which hovered on her lips, she knew instinctively that this was not the time, nor the place. Instead she asked:

'Does Félix le Clergé come here often?'

'Occasionally, when it is necessary to discuss certain laboratory tests.'

'He seems very nice,' she tried again.

'If you happen to like his particular brand of charm,' Paul replied scathingly, flicking his cigarette into the fire before glancing at her speculatively. Once again she noticed that peculiar tightness about his mouth.

'Well, I wouldn't know much about that,' she smiled up at him with a mischievous glint in her eyes. 'I only know that a certain gentleman by the name of Paul de Meillon has more than enough charm for me, thank you.'

Paul slipped an arm about her waist and held her close, while with the other hand he tilted her face upwards. There was an urgency in his manner which did not entirely escape her.

'Do you love me, Catherine?'

There it was again. The quest for confirmation

which was fast becoming an obsession. The uncertainty he exuded, reaching out and engulfing her, until that all too familiar trickle of fear shivered up her spine.

'Why do you doubt me so?' she counter-questioned, watching the muscles working in his cheek.

Paul released her suddenly. After several weeks of lying dormant, his doubts had reappeared, like a serpent raising its ugly head to spread its venom.

'You cannot tell me that you did not find Félix attractive?'

'But of course he's attractive,' Catherine admitted honestly. 'A woman would have to be blind not to notice that. He's charming, attentive ... and extremely French. I am sure that women must find him irresistible, although I can't say that a man like that would appeal to me particularly.'

'He is a man who is noted for his affairs. An amorist ... a Don Juan.' Paul lit another cigarette and paced the floor. 'There have been so many women in his life, I have lost count. He cannot leave an attractive woman alone, and they cannot, apparently, resist him.' He drew hard on his cigarette. 'You are an attractive woman, Catherine. *Very* attractive. What was he talking to you about while he was being so attentive this evening?'

Was this a display of jealousy? Or mere curiosity?

'We talked about nothing in particular. He asked me how I liked Paris, and whether I missed the warm South African climate. He asked me if I was by any chance a nurse, and when I told him that I had a degree in literature, he appeared to be very interested. He obviously wanted to ask more about it when he noticed how you were all watching us with disapproval written all over your faces ... and that's when he excused himself and returned to his chair.'

There was anger in her heart as she spoke, and for some indefinable reason she felt the desire to protect Félix le Clergé ... an action she was to regret later on.

'Félix was charming and friendly,' she continued. 'Not once did I get the impression that he was trying to flirt with me. On the contrary, I felt certain that he was slightly withdrawn.'

'Félix? Withdrawn? *Nom de dieu!* You must be out of your mind!' Paul exclaimed, flinging his half smoked cigarette into the grate. 'Félix has never been withdrawn as far as women are concerned, but perhaps he is making use of different tactics, for which you have obviously fallen. *Bonne nuit!*'

With that last remark flung over his shoulder, Paul stormed from the room, leaving Catherine to wonder what had motivated him to extend an invitation to Félix le Clergé when he so obviously disliked the man.

They had just had their first tiff, Catherine realized sadly as she subsided into a chair, and stared at the ashes in the grate. It was their first, but it certainly would not be their last, she realized unhappily.

CHAPTER SEVEN

PAUL had already left the house when Catherine awoke the following morning. Her eyes automatically searched for his customary note on the bedside table, but finding nothing she bathed and dressed in an effort to shake off her fit of depression. She had no idea what time Paul had come to bed the previous night. She had lain awake for what seemed like hours, waiting for him, until she could fight the tiredness no longer. If only she had the opportunity to speak to him this morning, she thought, for she had been nervous and edgy the previous evening and had perhaps said too much.

Adèle was at the breakfast table when Catherine entered.

'Paul left some time ago,' she told Catherine before biting into a buttered roll. 'I shall have to hurry as well or I shall be late this morning.'

Catherine decided on a piece of thinly sliced toast. She had not yet acquired the taste for the small bread rolls Paul and Adèle were so fond of.

'Do you know Félix le Clergé well?' she asked eventually as she poured herself a cup of strong black coffee.

Adèle's expression became guarded. 'Not very well – why?'

'I just wondered,' Catherine replied casually. An uneasy silence settled between them and remained until Adèle gulped down the remains of her coffee and excused herself hastily.

Adèle's haste was not entirely due to the lateness of the hour, Catherine realized, and she was left with no doubt in her mind that her assumption had been correct. Adèle knew Félix le Clergé far better than she wished to convey, and for some obscure reason she was determined to remain silent about it.

Paul would most certainly object to such a friendship between his sister and the man he had branded a Don Juan, she realized, as a feeling of pity overwhelmed her for the young girl she had come to think of with affection. What an impossible situation it must be for Adèle as well as for Félix. Was he truly a Don Juan as Paul had called him? she wondered. And if so, what could there be for Adèle in such a relationship, except heartache?

Susan Dunbury telephoned later that morning. 'I'm going into town this afternoon and I wondered whether you would like to accompany me,' she asked. 'I could show you a few places where one could pick up a bargain, seeing that you don't know Paris very well.'

Catherine accepted her offer gladly. It would at least be something to look forward to, and besides that, it would be a temporary relief from her own problems.

'I'll pick you up just after two,' Susan concluded their conversation.

Catherine spent the rest of the morning writing letters, one of which was to her father. She was careful, however, not to mention anything concerning the slight argument she and Paul had had, and kept the letter as lighthearted as possible.

Paul did not return home for lunch that day and neither had Catherine expected him to. He usually had a snack at the Clinic and quite often missed even that when he was operating. This had perturbed Catherine at first, for Paul had waved aside her protestations that he should make a point of eating something at midday.

He usually had a cup of coffee and sandwiches in between spells in the theatre, he had told her, and with that the subject was closed.

In spite of this knowledge, Catherine had hoped that Paul would, for once, make an exception to the rule and come home for lunch, if only to rid herself of the feeling that a wedge had suddenly been driven between them. She so desperately wanted to alleviate the harshness of their slight disagreement.

True to her word, Susan Dunbury arrived soon after two that afternoon and Catherine shelved her problems as they set out on an afternoon's shopping spree. Susan took Catherine to places she would never have found on her own, and although she had not intended buying anything, she returned home later that afternoon with a silk creation which not only enhanced the beautiful contours of her young figure, but made a sizeable dent in her bank balance.

'How I wish I could wear something like that,' Susan remarked with a sigh as Catherine slipped on the evening gown to examine herself in the mirror. 'I'm so skinny that it would be a waste hanging a beautiful thing like that on my bones.'

Catherine met Susan's envious glance in the mirror and noticed once again her delicately framed figure. Despite Susan's derogatory remarks about herself, Catherine was certain that her slenderness allowed her to look well-dressed in almost anything.

Running her hands over her hips and feeling the softness of the silk beneath her fingertips, Catherine remained hesitant about purchasing such a luxurious garment.

'Come on, Catherine. Be a devil and take it,' Susan urged.

The saleslady nodded profusely and uttered something in French which Susan apparently agreed with.

'*Madame*,' she said, turning to meet Catherine's inquiring glance. 'I am just telling Madame Dunbury that you must have the dress. It is made for you. *Certainement!*'

That did it! Catherine returned home with the costly creation, joyously anticipating Paul's reactions when he saw her in that magnificent gown for the first time.

It was after five when Susan dropped her at the house. The telephone was ringing in the hall and, dropping her parcel on to a chair, she hurriedly lifted the receiver. It was Paul.

'Where have you been?' his voice came accusingly over the line. 'I have been telephoning for the past hour.'

'I went shopping with Susan Dunbury this afternoon, and arrived home this very minute,' Catherine explained warily.

In his office at the Clinic, Paul wondered at the truth of this statement. He had spent a wretched night and an even more wretched day, and when the servants told him that Catherine was not at home, his mind had conjured up various uncomplimentary situations in which Catherine could be involved. Félix le Clergé, he knew, was in his laboratory, and had been there all afternoon. But there were others, he told himself, who would be only too willing to oblige. *Dieu!* His jaw hardened and his grip on the receiver increased considerably. Was he going mad to allow his doubts to play such havoc with his common sense?

'Paul?' Catherine questioned hesitantly as the silence lengthened. Something was wrong, she could feel the vibrations across the line covering the distance between them.

'I shall be home late this evening,' his voice finally reached her ears. 'I have to go into the theatre within a few minutes. Do not wait for me.'

'I'll keep your dinner in the warming oven.'

'*Merci.*'

'Paul?' Once again Catherine was hesitant, yet she had to satisfy herself that all was well between them. 'You're not angry with me for some reason, are you?'

'This is not the time to discuss such matters,' he said briskly before ringing off.

Left standing with the lifeless receiver in her hand, Catherine frowned. But there was no time to ponder over Paul's unusual behaviour, for Adèle arrived home soon afterwards, and her bubbling enthusiasm concerning the activities at her boutique swept aside Catherine's concern for Paul.

After dinner, Catherine wandered listlessly about the house. There was much that she could do, yet in her agitated state of mind she could not settle down to anything. Adèle was upstairs in her room going over several sketches for the spring selection, when Catherine heard a car come up the driveway.

Curious to know who could be paying them a visit at this early hour in the evening, Catherine was already on her way to the door when the doorbell chimed.

'Why, Monsieur le Clergé!' Catherine exclaimed in surprise as she discovered Félix, tall, dark and immaculately attired, standing on the doorstep. 'Do come in.'

'*Merci, madame.* I hope I am not disturbing you?'

'Not at all,' Catherine smiled as she stepped aside for him to enter, wondering at the same time to what she owed the unexpectedness of this visit.

Félix's glance swept passed her and the light in his eyes was unmistakable. '*Bon soir*, Adèle.'

Catherine turned sharply to find the younger girl standing at the foot of the stairs, her one hand clutching the banister tightly. Her anxious eyes darted from Félix to Catherine and back again.

'Oh, hello,' she said ungraciously. 'What are you doing here?'

Félix smiled indulgently. 'I knew that Paul would be delayed at the Clinic, so I have come to see Madame de Meillon. I hope she will be able to help me.'

'Help you?' Catherine asked, bewildered. 'I don't understand?'

'I do not think that Félix really has something to discuss with you, Cathy,' Adèle intervened, coming forward hastily and giving Félix a meaningful, persuasive look. 'Perhaps he has changed his mind. Not so, Félix?'

For several seconds the atmosphere was tense as two wills clashed in silent battle. It was Félix who finally spoke.

'*Non*, Adèle,' he insisted gently, 'I have not changed my mind, *chérie*.'

'Look, you two, we can't stand here on the doorstep arguing. Come inside, Félix – I may call you Félix?' Catherine interposed quickly. 'Come into the living-room so that we can sort out whatever it is in comfort.'

But Adèle remained argumentative. 'Cathy, it would be better if—'

'Adèle!' Catherine silenced her quietly and decisively. 'I'm not a complete idiot. There's something the matter and I know it. I realized it last night and I'm even more sure of it now. Let Félix tell me what it is and then, if I can help, I'll do so gladly.'

'*Merci, madame*. You are most kind,' Félix thanked her as they entered the living-room and seated themselves.

'Please. Before we start . . . do call me Catherine.'

'*Merci*, Catherine, it will make it so much easier.'

'Well?' she prompted as a silence threatened.

'I do not quite know where to start,' Félix confessed, fetching out his cigarette case and lighting one of his cheroots with unsteady fingers.

'The beginning is always the best place,' she smiled encouragingly.

'*Oui*, the beginning,' he nodded, blowing a stream of smoke towards the ceiling. 'You are aware that I do not have a very good reputation?'

'So my husband painstakingly informed me. Yes.'

'Ah!' he smiled then, a bitter, twisted smile that wrenched her heart. 'I thought so. Catherine, I am not going to make excuses for myself, but if you should be able to assist us – me, then I must tell you all there is to know about myself.' He hesitated for a moment, glancing at Adèle, who sat fidgeting on Catherine's left, before continuing. 'I do not know my father. I have never met him. He left my mother when I was only a small baby, and after that my mother had many men. She became a bad woman, a . . .' He appeared to find difficulty in deciding on the correct word.

'Prostitute?' Catherine supplied calmly.

'*Oui*,' he nodded hastily. 'That is how she made her money, and how she paid for my education. I was sent to a private school in the South of France, and although I spent my holidays with my mother, she was too busy with her men friends to be concerned about me. When she could spare the time, it was only to impress upon my mind that I must take out of life all that I could get, and that I must not ever fool myself that there was such a thing as . . . love. Love, she said, was only another nice word for desire.'

Félix stared at the tip of his cheroot frowningly, and at that moment Catherine felt pitifully sorry for him. What a ghastly environment for any child to grow up in, and to pattern his future life on.

'This I believed,' Félix continued slowly, 'for not once did she contradict that statement. Indeed, she continued stressing it. As I grew older, I began to live my life as she did hers. There have been many women in my life, Catherine. I cannot even remember all their names. Perhaps, if I should see them again, I might not even recognize them. I took what I could from life, and I enjoyed it. It was by then part of my nature. The women were satisfied and so, I thought, was I. Until . . . until I met Adèle.'

'Félix, please!' Adèle interrupted agitatedly. 'It will do no good!'

'Adèle, I *must* speak,' Félix insisted harshly. 'You know as well as I do that we cannot go on and on this way. We are getting nowhere.'

As Adèle settled down grudgingly, Félix continued once more. 'From the moment I met Adèle, here at Château de Bonheur on one of my rare visits, I realized that what I had always believed was not so. There *was* such a thing as love. I love Adèle and she, in spite of my reputation, loves me. I do not need those other women now, and I never will again. I wish only to have Adèle as my own. I respect her, and want to take care of her. *Dieu!* I swear that I will never shame her or harm her. I do not want a flirtation; a mistress. My intentions are honourable. I want her for my wife!' Félix crushed his cheroot into the ashtray with fierce movements. 'The only thing which stands in our way of happiness is . . .'

'Paul?' Catherine suggested as Félix hesitated.

'*Oui,*' he nodded. 'Adèle prefers that we should let

things ... ride, as they say. She is sure that Paul will eventually realize that I am no longer the gigolo he knew me to be, and that he will then not mind so much if I pay attention to his sister.'

'And you don't somehow think this will work?' asked Catherine.

'*Non.* I know it will not. Once a man has a reputation, it clings to him for the rest of his life. I say we must speak to Paul, but Adèle does not want this. What do you advise, Catherine?'

Catherine thought for a moment selfishly of her own problems. If Félix approached Paul and confided in him it would certainly alleviate the pressure of her own situation, for Paul was not a harsh man by nature. Had she not herself experienced his gentleness and understanding after he had saved her from spending the rest of her life in a wheelchair? What advice should she give Félix? she wondered desperately.

She glanced from Adèle, who sat wringing her hands in her lap, a troubled look in her dark eyes, to Félix, who sat waiting expectantly for her to answer. He, too, looked troubled, but there was no doubt in her mind about the depth of his feelings for Adèle. Surely Paul would not be so blinded by the man's reputation that he would not be able to see the truth in Félix's eyes; his very attitude, for it was so clearly evident to her at that moment.

'I think you're right, Félix,' Catherine said eventually, with the firm conviction that she had made the correct decision. 'You *should* speak to Paul. He is not a man without compassion or understanding, and it will certainly be to your advantage.'

'No! Paul will not understand! I know, I know!' Adèle cried, getting to her feet and pacing the floor as though she was no longer able to restrain herself. 'He has never made any secret as to what he thinks of Félix. In the past he has always criticized my friends. No one has been good enough.' She faced them then, her eyes pleading. 'Oh, Cathy, please understand. Paul has not been harsh. He is a wonderful brother, but he can be too protective; too critical. If he has not approved of the other young men who have taken me out a few times, then I cannot see him approving of Félix.'

'But Paul doesn't realize, or even know of the circumstances—'

'No, no, no!' Adèle interrupted her almost hysterically. 'Paul must *not* know! Not yet!' She clutched Catherine's arm fiercely, the anguish clearly noticeable on her face. 'Please, Cathy ... Félix ... give it a little more time. Let Paul see for himself how Félix has changed. As soon as I notice a difference in Paul's attitude, I will tell him the truth. Please, please!'

Catherine glanced questioningly at Félix. He shrugged his shoulders with hopeless resignation. Like herself, he was a little bit older and a little bit wiser, and they both knew that it would not be as easy as Adèle predicted.

'Very well, Adèle,' Catherine conceded gently. 'If you feel so strongly about it, then there's nothing else we can do.'

'And you will keep our secret?' she begged anxiously.

'Yes, I will keep your secret.'

'Oh, Cathy, you are wonderful!' she cried, hugging Catherine thankfully.

'I'm sorry, Félix,' Catherine spoke gently over Adèle's shoulder.

'I am sorry too, but I can wait,' he stated firmly. 'For Adèle I will wait for ever, if I have to.'

Catherine sat curled up in a chair in front of the log fire, with a book on her lap. She had tried to read, but her thoughts were too preoccupied with Félix and Adèle to concentrate on anything. When Paul finally arrived home, there was an aura of cold reserve about him which prohibited her from rushing into his arms, and this hurt her far more than he would ever realize.

'You must be tired,' she observed as he dropped into the chair opposite her. 'Greta has kept your dinner in the warming oven. Would you like to eat now, or later?'

'Later,' he said, lighting himself a cigarette. 'First, you can tell me what you have been doing all day.'

'Nothing much. It's been a long, lonely day without you,' she replied in an effort to break through his reserve. And then, almost accusingly, 'You left before I woke this morning.'

'Yes . . . so I did,' he observed slowly. 'You had no visitors?'

'No.'

This was the first time she had blatantly lied to Paul, she thought miserably as she fingered the pages of her book. How she wished she could have told him the truth.

'Then you have suddenly started smoking cheroots, perhaps?' he remarked cynically.

'Oh!' What a fool she had been not to empty the ashtray Félix had used, she chided herself as the colour suffused her face. 'Well . . . yes, I did have a visitor early this evening.'

'Félix le Clergé?' he guessed accurately. Félix was, after all, seldom without his cheroots.

'Yes.'

'And you were not going to tell me about it?'

Little sparks of anger glittered in Paul's eyes, and Catherine felt her own heartbeat quicken with something close to fear.

'I – I didn't think it was important.'

'So?' Paul got to his feet and flicked his cigarette angrily into the grate. 'A man like Félix, who has a reputation for seducing every woman he meets, visits you while I am away, and you consider it not important enough to mention the fact to me?'

'Paul, please!' Catherine threw her book aside and stood up. She was by now every bit as agitated as Paul. 'He merely came to – to thank me for the excellent dinner last night.'

Another little white lie, her conscience reminded her.

'That little errand would not have taken him more than a minute, yet he remained long enough to smoke one of his cheroots.' In the firelight his expression was uncommonly harsh, and it made Catherine think of one of those mediaeval conquerors she had seen in her history books at school. 'Can it be,' he continued, his eyes narrowed to slits, 'that you have fallen prey to his charm?'

'You're being ridiculous!'

'Am I?' Paul was suddenly very close to her. So close, in fact, that she could almost feel the anger vibrating through him. His mouth twisted sardonically as he looked down into her upturned face, and for a moment Catherine thought he was going to strike her as he lifted his hand, his nostrils flaring, his eyes a violent black. She closed her eyes tightly as she awaited the impact of his hand, and in that moment of stress, she realized the enormity of the promise Adèle had extracted from her. A promise of silence she had given in a moment of weakness; of pity, and which was already affecting her own happiness in a way she had never dreamed of.

Paul stepped back suddenly, as though he could not bear to be within touching distance of her. 'It has not taken you long to tire of me, has it? And Félix is such a suave lover, did you not discover?'

'Paul!' Her eyes flew open filled with incredulity.

The implication of his words left her trembling and bereft of further speech. What had she done to deserve his wrath, and more important, what had happened to the warm, friendly and understanding man she had married? This cool, mistrusting stranger was not the Paul she knew and loved, and it frightened her. She gestured pleadingly towards him, but Paul had already turned and was striding towards the door.

'I have work to do,' he informed her coldly.

'Your dinner—'

'Feed it to the dogs,' he snapped. 'I am not hungry. And, Catherine,' he turned to face her then and she shivered inwardly at the harshness of his expression, 'I do not wish to be disturbed.'

Catherine's hands had dropped lifelessly to her sides as she stood and watched him go. It was understandable that he should jump to the conclusion that she was having an affair with Félix, but surely, if he could not trust Félix, he knew that he could trust her? If only she could go to him with the truth, but her lips were sealed until Adèle freed her from that promise.

'Cathy?' She looked up sharply as Adèle anxiously entered the living-room moments later. 'You did not tell Paul? You kept your promise?'

'I didn't tell Paul,' Catherine answered mechanically. 'I kept my promise.'

'Oh, *merci, chérie. Merci!*' Catherine reeled under

the impact of Adèle's weight as she was clasped in a bear hug. 'Where is *mon frère* now?'

'In his study, and he does not wish to be disturbed.'

'There has been trouble?' Adèle asked quickly, a frown creasing her brow.

Catherine turned and stared into the fire, hiding her anguished expression from the younger girl. 'Paul unfortunately discovered that Félix had been here earlier this evening. We had a bit of a row, that's all.' What an understatement, she thought, calling their confrontation 'a bit of a row'!

'Paul is upset?'

'Upset?' She glanced at Adèle then, suppressing the feeling of slight hysteria within her. 'No, Paul isn't exactly upset. He just doesn't like the idea of Félix coming here when he's not at home, he is thoroughly displeased.'

'He is tired, perhaps,' Adèle suggested hopefully. 'Do not worry. When Paul is like this it is better to leave him alone. He will have forgotten it all in the morning, you will see.'

'I suppose so,' Catherine sighed doubtfully.

'What reason did you give for Félix's visit?'

'I said he had come to thank me for the dinner last night.'

'Cathy, you are a very dear friend and sister-in-law, and I thank you.' Adèle kissed Catherine lightly on the cheek. 'Good night, *chérie.*'

Catherine bade her good night, swallowing at the lump in her throat.

For the first time that night, Paul did not come to their bedroom. She heard him later in the room adjoining theirs, walking about restlessly until she eventually heard the bed creak, and saw the stretch of light under the door go off.

Catherine lay awake after that, unable to sleep. Her tears soaked the pillow as she tossed and turned until the early hours of the morning, when she finally slept from sheer exhaustion.

CHAPTER EIGHT

It was spring in Paris. There was something about this time of the year that imbued everyone with new vigour. Tender young leaves were sprouting on the trees, and the sweet scent of orange blossoms permeated the air.

All this Catherine noticed, while in her heart it remained winter. Paul had maintained his cool and aloof attitude since that fateful evening he had returned home to discover that Félix had visited her at the Château de Bonheur, and had remained longer than he had thought necessary. Relentlessly she had endeavoured to break through the wall of reserve he had erected between them, but to no avail. Her efforts were looked upon with cold suspicion and the only result she achieved was the widening of the gulf between them, and the painful knowledge that her bubble of happiness had burst all too soon.

Susan Dunbury had become a firm friend of Catherine's during this trying time, and it was to her that Catherine turned for advice.

'You must speak to Paul,' she advised one afternoon when Catherine had tea with her. 'You can't let this situation go on indefinitely.'

'How can I broach such a delicate subject when he hardly ever gives me the opportunity to be alone with him for more than a moment?' Catherine replied in anguish. 'He spends most of his time at the Clinic and when he's home he locks himself in his study until late at night. And then . . . I did promise Adèle—'

'Oh, nonsense,' Susan interrupted. 'Adèle should

never have extracted that promise from you. Can't she see what all this is doing to your marriage?'

'I'm afraid I've hidden the truth from her,' Catherine admitted, lowering her glance.

Susan shook her head sadly. 'Cathy, you're a very loyal person, but your loyalty should be to your husband, and not to his sister.'

'I realize that, but Adèle was so pathetically adamant about Paul not knowing that I was forced to give her my promise that I would remain silent.'

'Wait until I get hold of Adèle,' Susan said tight-lipped. 'I'll give her a piece of my mind.'

Catherine laughed suddenly, if only to relieve the tension for a moment. 'I'm sorry to have saddled you with my problems, Susan. It wasn't fair of me.'

'Nonsense!' she exclaimed crossly. 'What are friends for after all.'

On the way to the Château de Bonheur that afternoon, Catherine made a resolution that she would indeed make a point of speaking to Paul on his return from the medical conference he would be attending the following week. He had told her, quite indifferently, that he would be away for three or four days, and she was glad now to have those few days to herself during which she would be able to rehearse carefully what she had to tell him. She hoped that he would be in a more receptive mood after his return from London, and not as unapproachable as he had been lately.

As the time drew near for Paul's departure, Catherine became increasingly anxious for the opportunity to clear the air between them. It would be useless speaking to Paul before the conference, for he was quite morose. Breaking her promise to Adèle was not going to be easy, but as Susan had reminded her, her loyalty should be to her husband. Once he knew the truth, he would realize that his doubts were unfounded, and he would be able to handle the existing situation between Félix and Adèle far better than she ever could.

Adèle was not happy about her deception either, Catherine realized. Like any other girl she wanted to be openly courted by the man she loved, yet the fear of Paul denouncing Félix was far greater than her desire to make her love known to her brother. These unnatural circumstances were taking their toll, Catherine noticed with considerable concern, for Adèle was becoming pale and withdrawn.

On the eve of Paul's departure for England to attend the medical conference, he surprised Catherine by entering their bedroom again for the first time in weeks. Dressed in a silk dressing gown over his pyjamas, he entered the room through the interleading door and stood for a moment scowling at her from beneath his heavy eyebrows.

Acutely conscious of the fact that she was clad only in a filmy négligé, Catherine stopped brushing her hair and averted her face, mainly to hide her flushed cheeks from his prying eyes.

'Did you want to see me about something, Paul?' she asked eventually as the silence lengthened uncomfortably.

Paul shook himself slightly. He had been staring, he realized, but she had never seemed more desirable than in that moment. She had brushed her hair until it was feathery and curled softly about her face. Her eyes held a gentle appeal, while her lips were slightly parted. He noticed the transparency of the négligé covering the gentle curves of her figure, and his heartbeats quickened as he remembered the warm softness of her body in his arms.

'Paul?' she questioned again, fighting down the panic she felt.

'I – I shall be leaving before breakfast tomorrow morning,' he told her, and to his own ears his voice sounded strange. 'I thought I should tell you.'

'Oh.' He had never bothered recently to inform her of his intentions, so why now? she wondered.

There was a tenseness in the air which Catherine could not explain. After announcing his intentions, she had expected Paul to leave ... but he remained, looking at her with that peculiar, almost questioning look in his eyes. A pulse throbbed painfully in her neck as they stood facing each other ... waiting. There was a yearning now to breach the gap between them, although both were reluctant to make the first move.

It was Catherine who finally took an involuntary step forward, the brush dropping from her nerveless fingers to the carpeted floor. 'Paul?'

He needed no further encouragement, for in the next instant she was caught up in his embrace, the small softness of her crushed against the long hard line of his body. His mouth raked her neck, claimed her yielding lips in a soul-destroying kiss, and then moved down the length of her neck once more, pushing the shoulder strap of her nightdress aside with his questing hand as his lips caressed her.

'Oh, Paul, Paul, my darling,' she moaned softly as the familiar aching fire spread through her veins. The muscles in his shoulders moved beneath her fingers as she clung to him, surrendering unresistingly to his lovemaking and rejoicing in the possibility that this would bring to an end the weeks of agony she had endured.

With a muttered exclamation and heavily thudding heart, Paul lifted her in his arms and carried her within the shadow of the drapes.

The breeze sighed through the chestnut trees, and drifted on. Then there was silence as nature waited for the new day to break.

Catherine awoke the following morning with a sense of well-being. She uncurled, stretching lazily, and then, as memory returned, she turned her head sharply, only to discover that Paul had already gone. With a smile quivering on her lips, she stretched out an arm to take the note he had left her on his pillow.

Her expression sobered as she read through the note. Visibly pale and trembling, she sat upright and read it through once more in incredulous disbelief.

'Catherine,' Paul had written in his firm hand-writing, 'my apologies for last night. You were temptingly attractive, and I lost my head. I am, after all, only human, but it will not happen again. Paul.'

Her fingers curled convulsively about the note. He had lost his head, Paul had written. If it had been any other woman, would he have reacted in the same way? Did he have need of a woman last night? Just any woman? And, as she was so readily available, he had had no reason to search further?

These thoughts scorched through her mind and soul, and filled her with shame. What a fool she had been last night to think that Paul wished to re-establish their earlier relationship as much as she wished it! How naïve she had been in her presumption that he had finally realized the error of his judgment.

Catherine looked about her wildly. How was she going to get through these few days until Paul returned? she wondered. Already the walls of the Château de Bonheur appeared to be crowding in on her. 'Château of Happiness'. What a mockery that name was, for her happiness had been all too brief in

137

this magnificent home.

When she walked past the breakfast room an hour later, Adèle called to her.

'Are you not having breakfast this morning?'

'I'm not hungry.' Food would certainly choke her at that moment.

'Can I not even tempt you with coffee?' Adèle persisted.

Catherine hesitated a moment and then succumbed to the idea.

'Is something the matter?' Adèle asked when she saw Catherine's hand tremble as she held the coffee pot.

'Just a slight headache,' Catherine prevaricated. 'I thought a walk in the garden would clear it.'

'Paul called me early this morning and asked me to take him to the airport. He left you these.'

Adèle dropped a small bunch of keys on the table beside Catherine's cup.

'The keys for the Bentley?'

'Oui. Paul said not to worry. He will take a taxi from the airport on his return.'

'I see . . .'

Was this part of the apology, Catherine wondered, being entrusted with the keys to the Bentley? She was suddenly bristling with helpless anger. How dared he treat her this way!

'You can drive the Bentley, can you not?' Adèle asked suddenly.

'Yes, I've driven it on a few occasions. I normally take the bus, though.'

'You should ask Paul to buy you a small Mini like mine.'

'Perhaps.'

'What are you going to do today?' Adèle asked.

'Oh . . . I haven't thought. There is very little to do

138

in the house, the servants are all so efficient. I might just supervise the evening meal, but as it's only the two of us, I shall tell Greta not to make anything too elaborate.'

'I shall not be dining with you this evening, Cathy. Félix has invited me out to dinner.'

'Oh.'

Now that the cat is away, the mice can play more freely, Catherine thought wryly.

'I'm sorry,' Adèle interrupted her thoughts.

'Don't let it bother you. I'll just have something light and then go to bed with a book.'

'You could come with us.'

'Don't be silly,' Catherine snapped irritably, and then continued more gently, 'There's an old English saying, "Two's company, three's a crowd". I would never dream of spoiling the few hours you'll have alone together.'

Adèle finished her breakfast in subdued silence, while Catherine poured herself another cup of coffee.

'I must leave you now,' Adèle said eventually, slipping into her coat and taking her handbag. 'Enjoy your day.'

Enjoy your day. The words echoed through Catherine's mind long after Adèle had gone. Enjoy your day! Yes, she thought cynically and perilously close in tears, she shall certainly enjoy her day, and the next few days for that matter, after that cryptic little note Paul had left her, and the implication of those ill-chosen words.

With a feeling of utter despair, she took the keys Adèle had tossed unceremoniously at her, and hurried upstairs to renew her make-up and collect her handbag. A day in the country would do her the world of good, she decided as she pulled a comb through her hair. Why not? There was no one to stop her, and certainly no one who cared or needed her at the Château de Bonheur.

Deciding on the first road that took her fancy, Catherine drove at a leisurely pace to nowhere in particular. She had no fear of losing her way, for there were prominent signposts at various strategic points which one could hardly avoid noticing. It was nevertheless a lonely trip, and she was not in the proper mood to enjoy the countryside as it came alive after the long winter. After enjoying a light lunch in a small village, she decided to return home. It would be far better being lonely in familiar surroundings than to have people eyeing her speculatively and wondering what a woman was doing driving about on her own.

That night Catherine lay tossing in her bed. Sleep evaded her in the silence and desolation of the empty house. Never before had she felt as lonely as at that moment, with nothing but a deserted house and her own unhappy thoughts to keep her company. The servants had long since retired to their homes, leaving an all enveloping silence behind.

It was after eleven when she heard a car come up the driveway, and after a few moments the subdued voices of Félix and Adèle downstairs. Finally she heard the front door being securely locked and the car's lights swept past her window as it turned and left the way it had come.

There was a tentative knock on her bedroom door. 'Catherine, are you awake?'

'Come in, Adèle,' Catherine called, snapping on the bedside lamp.

The door opened and Adèle entered hesitantly. 'You have not been asleep?'

'No.' She patted the side of the bed. 'Come and sit

down, then you can tell me about your evening.'

'Oh, Cathy!' Adèle sighed ecstatically, subsiding on to the bed. 'It was such a lovely evening. Félix took me to a small restaurant for dinner. We danced a bit, and later we just sat and talked and talked.'

How seldom they must have the opportunity to meet each other like this, Catherine thought sadly. 'Paul does not often go away, so how do you manage to see each other when he is at home?'

'There is a small café which belongs to friends of Félix,' Adèle explained. 'They are an elderly couple and they will not talk. We meet there for lunch sometimes, or just for a quick cup of coffee in their private little kitchen.'

Catherine smiled to herself, and nodded. How ingenious their method of meeting!

'Shall we go down to the kitchen and make ourselves a glass of warm milk?' she suggested eventually.

'*Oui*, that will be nice,' Adèle agreed.

The day ended quite pleasantly after all, as they sat beside the kitchen table sipping their warm milk. They had become so engrossed in conversation that when the hall clock struck one o'clock, they looked at each other in disbelief.

'You must get to bed, Adèle, or you will be worthless tomorrow morning,' Catherine observed as she rinsed the glasses and left them on the rack to dry.

'I do not want this night to end,' Adèle sighed reluctantly.

'I know, my dear,' Catherine kissed her lightly on the cheek, 'but now it's time for bed.'

'*Bonne nuit*, Cathy,' Adèle whispered as they parted company.

'*Bonne nuit*,' Catherine echoed.

The evening before Paul's return Félix called to see Adèle. Catherine left them in the living-room together while she retired to her room to do a few quick alterations to the hem of one of her long evening dresses. Later, on her way down to the kitchen to press the hem of her dress, she was surprised to hear raised voices coming from the living-room. Adèle and Félix were obviously having an argument, of which Catherine could not understand a word, as they were speaking rapidly in French.

As she reached the hallway, the living-room door flew open and Adèle rushed out and ran past her in a tearful state.

'What happened?' Catherine asked Félix moments after she heard Adèle's bedroom door slam shut.

Félix pushed his hands into his pockets and hunched his shoulders. 'It is the same argument we always have,' he explained. 'I want that we should talk to Paul, but Adèle refuses. What must I do?'

It was an awkward situation which affected not only the lives of Félix and Adèle, but Catherine's as well. She could not tell Félix of her intention to speak to Paul on his return, for she could not say when she would have the opportunity, or whether Paul would be willing to listen to her.

'Give her time,' she suggested slowly.

'Time?' Félix exploded. 'Time? There has been enough time wasted!'

'I know, but—'

'Catherine, we cannot go on like this!' Félix said, gesturing imploringly with his hands.

'I agree with you, Félix. You cannot go on like this.'

Catherine swivelled round wide-eyed, to find Paul standing in the doorway, his one hand resting on the door frame. Her heart was thundering so loudly she was certain that the neighbours could hear.

'Paul, I didn't expect you so soon!' Of all the words she could have chosen, those were the most ill-fated.

'No, I am certain you did not,' Paul agreed coldly. 'How regretful that I should spoil this delightful little *tête-à-tête* by returning so unexpectedly.'

'Paul, it is not what—' Catherine and Félix started speaking together, and stopped midway, glancing at each other.

'Perhaps you'd better go, Félix,' Catherine said quickly before he said more than was intended.

'But I—'

'Please, Félix. Go!' she pleaded urgently.

'Yes, Félix,' Paul echoed sarcastically, standing aside. 'Please go so that I may speak to my . . . *wife*,' he stressed the word cynically, 'privately, and without interruption. Go, also, before I lose my temper and throw you out!'

Félix cast a troubled look in Catherine's direction, but when she gestured once more that he should leave, he turned and strode from the room. He only hoped that Catherine would be unharmed, for he had never before seen Paul in such a thunderous mood.

Paul closed the living-room door and stood with his back against it, his arms folded across his broad chest. The silence which hung in the room was explosive, and Catherine quivered inwardly. She must remain calm, she told herself, or the situation could develop into something beyond repair.

Glancing at the evening dress she was clutching in her hands, Paul said: 'It appears you were going out.'

'No, I—'

'How dare you! *Nom de dieu,* how dare you!' Paul

raged, coming towards her menacingly. 'How dare you carry on your . . . affair here in my house!'

'But, Paul, I—'

'You must have been only too happy that I would be away for a few days so that you could spend your time with Félix without fearing that I would find out.'

'You don't know what you're saying,' she gasped, striving for calmness as he towered over her, his eyes black with rage, his lips drawn into a thin line of disapproval. 'I realize that Félix being here looks as though—'

'Do you think I cannot see what is going on right under my nose? Do you think I am a fool?'

'Paul, I know what you're thinking, but—'

'I tell you this, Catherine,' he interrupted in a voice that sent little shivers of fear up her spine. 'I thought I could trust you, but it appears that I cannot. I knew that I should not have married you, but very cunningly,' he laughed cynically with more than a trace of bitterness in his voice, 'yes, very cunningly you made me believe that you loved me. I was convinced because, for once, I let my heart rule my head. But it did not take you very long to tire of me, did it? *Did* it?'

He took her by the shoulders then and shook her until she felt her neck would snap. Her evening dress lay on the floor in a crumpled heap, forgotten in this moment of stress when it had slipped from her arm during his onslaught.

'Please, Paul, let me explain,' she begged, tears stinging her eyes from the pain he was inflicting upon her.

'Explain?' Paul released her with a gesture of disgust. 'What is there to explain? Lies! That is what I shall get from you. Lies! But I tell you this also, I shall not divorce you so that you can go to Félix. You are married to me and you shall stay that way. And one other thing, do not bring your ... *affaires* home. Be a little more discreet in future.'

That stung Catherine into anger.

'You have no right to speak to me in this way!'

'I have every right to speak to my insubordinate wife in any manner I please.'

'Insubordinate?' she gasped. 'I don't suppose it's occurred to you that you could be wrong?'

Paul laughed cynically. 'Félix is not the kind of man who visits a woman to pass the time of day by discussing the weather.'

'You don't know the true facts, and you refuse to give me the opportunity to explain.'

'I do not wish to hear more lies.'

'Darn you, Paul! It's Adèle whom Félix loves and whom he came to see,' she blurted out.

Flustered and angry, she had been driven on by desperation, and had blundered out the truth, not at all in the way she had planned. She despised herself for allowing Paul to shatter the calm she had striven to obtain, but there was now no turning back. Those words had been uttered and were taking effect.

White to the lips, Paul faced her silently. If she had struck him physically it could not have had a more devastating effect. The ridiculous desire to hold him comfortingly in her arms took possession of her, a desire to ward off the blow she herself had delivered.

'You are lying!' Paul said in a harsh whisper.

The next moment he turned on his heel and jerked open the door. He crossed the hall in a few long strides and took the steps two at a time. If Catherine was speaking the truth he would have it out with Adèle here and now.

Adèle's door was closed and without bothering to

knock he flung it open with a violence that almost wrenched it from its hinges, and stood for a moment breathing heavily as Adèle sat up in bed with a fearful expression on her face.

'Is it true?' he demanded in French. 'Is it true that you and Félix are in love with each other, and that he came to visit *you* this evening and not Catherine? Do not lie to me, Adèle,' he implored, a little calmer now as he approached the bed. 'There have been enough lies in this house. I want the truth.'

Adèle struggled with herself. She realized for the first time what extensive harm she had caused by extracting that promise of silence from Catherine. And Catherine, dear loyal Catherine, had kept that promise regardless of the unhappiness it had brought about. She had heard them arguing in the living-room and as Paul's voice was raised she was able to follow and understand. For Catherine's sake she should admit the truth, yet the look on Paul's face frightened her. There would be no reasoning with him while he was in this mood.

'I am sorry, *mon frère*, but there is no truth in that statement.'

Catherine paced the floor while awaiting Paul's return. Adèle would never forgive her, she was sure. But she had not intended telling him in this way. If only Félix had not been here this evening. If only . . . ! What a futile thought, she chided herself angrily.

When Paul finally re-entered the living-room, his face was ashen and there were tired lines about his mouth. His suffering was as great as hers, she knew, but in this matter they could not help each other while Paul obstinately believed his own theories.

'So you have lied again.'

Catherine's heart gave a jolt and she clutched at the back of a chair for support.

'You are a woman without shame,' he continued coldly. 'I never thought you could be like this, Catherine. That you could have the audacity to involve my sister in your sordid affair goes beyond the stretch of my imagination. I think I despise you!'

'Paul, no!' she breathed, a sickening feeling at the pit of her stomach as Paul turned and left the room.

'Paul, please wait!' she cried, almost stumbling in her effort to deter him.

'I do not wish to hear any more,' he said icily as he reached the outer door.

'Where are you going?'

'Out!' he shouted, slamming the door behind him and causing the sound to reverberate throughout the house.

Numbed in every limb, Catherine stood there staring at the door through which Paul had just disappeared. Oh, God! she thought helplessly, where do we go from here? What can I do? Who can I turn to for advice?

'Cathy?'

She turned wearily to find Adèle standing there, clutching her dressing gown about her slim waist.

'Cathy, I am sorry,' she cried, flinging herself into Catherine's arms with a sob. 'Forgive me. Please forgive me!'

'It's I who have to ask you to forgive me,' Catherine said, trying to comfort the younger girl. 'I broke my promise to you, but my intention was to break it to him gently, and not in the way I did. I allowed Paul to anger me, and spoilt it all. I'm afraid that finding Félix here this evening drove all reason from Paul, and—'

'Do not explain,' Adèle stopped her, 'I understand.'

'What are we going to do?' Catherine asked as they faced each other helplessly.

'I will tell Paul,' Adèle said, a determined look on her face. 'When he is not so angry I will tell him the truth. Give me just a little time to think about what I have to say.'

Yes, thought Catherine, Paul would listen to her. He had no reason to distrust her, and therefore he would accept her explanation with calm understanding.

A dull ache settled in her throat. How she wished she could cry, but what would tears help in a situation like this? To whom could she go for comfort and understanding? Susan Dunbury? No, she decided, she could not burden Susan further with her problems.

Old Sarah's prediction on that morning she had driven out to Franschhoek with Paul suddenly came to Catherine, its meaning stunningly clear.

'You have heartache ahead of you. He's a man who thinks with his head and not his heart. He'll never believe that you really love him, and that you're not just being grateful for all he's done for you.'

'Be patient,' Sarah had also said, and Catherine sighed heavily. She would have to learn to be patient, no matter how difficult it would become.

CHAPTER NINE

In his office at the Clinic, Paul worked feverishly for the next hour. There was a large amount of paper work that had to be done, and being away for three days had increased the size of the pile considerably.

When he had left the house earlier that evening, he had been in a furious rage. He had always prided himself on being a good judge of character in the past, but he had failed abominably as far as Catherine was concerned. He should have realized at the time that she was as young and impressionable as he had thought, and that she would be incapable of discerning between love and gratitude. How he loathed that word gratitude!

He had allowed her to convince him of her love at a time when his emotions had overruled his common sense, and he despised himself for it. It was logical, therefore, that when she tired of him she would turn to a man like Félix, who was always available to a beautiful woman who had become bored with her husband.

Paul flung his pen across the desk and stood up. It was impossible to work with such distressing thoughts chasing through his mind. For years now he had known of Félix's amorous adventures, and yet Catherine expected him to believe otherwise. Of course they were having an affair! What else would Félix have been visiting Catherine for? Paul thought stubbornly.

He had never thought that Catherine would be so vile as to suggest that it was Adèle whom Félix had called to see. Adèle was not at all the kind of woman to attract a man like Félix. But then neither was Catherine. *Bon dieu!* He did not know any more what to think. The thought of another man holding Catherine in his arms and making love to her made him want to commit murder! She is mine! Paul thought ferociously. She is mine and she shall stay that way!

It was late when Paul finally arrived home that evening. He found the living-room light still on, and on the floor beside a chair lay the dress Catherine had been holding when he had arrived so unexpectedly. Picking it up, he held it in his hands and stood staring at it for a moment. Then, with anguished exclamation, he pressed his face into the soft material, breathing in the hint of perfume which still clung to the material. Perfume which he had brought for her as a gift from Grasse, and which he had given to her on the day he had asked her to marry him.

A glint of metal caught his eye and on examining the dress closer, he discovered a needle pinned to the hem, a thread of cotton still attached to it. Had she been working on the dress when he had arrived earlier that evening? It was obvious now that she had not intended wearing the dress. And Félix? Could his visit have been purely platonic?

'We cannot go on like this,' he remembered Félix saying as he entered the living-room. What could that have meant other than that he and Catherine could not continue meeting each other in such a secretive fashion? Adèle? No, he told himself fiercely, in spite of Catherine's insinuations, he could not believe that Adèle was involved. She had been, after all, in bed when he arrived, he told himself, and who would know her better than he himself?

He was trying, unsuccessfully, to find a loophole for

Catherine, he knew. Trying to find some other explanation for Félix's presence in his home earlier that evening, but he could think of none.

Paul dropped the dress on to the chair and stalked out of the room, switching off the light as he went.

Tomorrow, he decided firmly, he would speak to Félix and demand to know the truth. But what could he expect to hear? he thought dejectedly as he entered his room. Félix would merely deny everything, and what proof had he, Paul, that his assumption was correct? If he had caught them embracing, it would of course alter matters. No, it would perhaps be far better to wait and make sure before he went into action, Paul decided eventually. He was, perhaps, a little afraid of the truth?

Catherine flung herself into doing the household chores, much to the dismay of the staff. Even Greta raised a fair eyebrow when Catherine finally marched into the kitchen one morning.

'You are not well, *madame*?' she asked with suspicious amusement as Catherine helped peel the potatoes and plan the evening meal.

'Greta, if I don't do something, I shall go mad in this enormous house with no one to talk to but the portraits of Monsieur de Meillon's forefathers, who do nothing but glare down at me from the walls.'

The hint of desperation in her voice was clearly audible to Greta's sensitive ears. Although she would never dream of prying into Madame's affairs, she could not help but wonder what had brought about the unhappy, strained look in Madame's eyes.

It was one morning, while having a cup of tea with Greta in the kitchen, that the telephone rang.

'I shall answer it, *madame*,' Greta offered, and disappeared swiftly into the hall only to return a few seconds later. 'It is for you, *madame*. It is Monsieur Félix from the Clinic.'

Filled with apprehension, Catherine took the call. 'Hello, Félix.' She spoke softly into the receiver while at the same time glancing guiltily over her shoulder, almost as though she expected Paul to appear suddenly in the doorway.

'*Bonjour*, Catherine. I am sorry to trouble you,' Félix said quickly. 'I have been worried about you and must speak with you. Could you have lunch with me today?'

'I don't know,' she replied slowly, suddenly afraid of the repercussions such an action could evoke.

'Please, Catherine. The telephone . . . I cannot talk here,' he said urgently.

'Very well, Félix,' she agreed after a moment's hesitation, wondering what it was that Félix had to discuss with her so urgently. 'Where and at what time?'

He mentioned a restaurant close to the Etoile, knowing that she would find it with little trouble. 'Will twelve-thirty suit you?'

'Yes, Félix, I'll be there,' she agreed, ignoring the warning bell that rang somewhere in her subconscious.

At twelve-thirty exactly, Catherine entered the restaurant, and her stomach instantly twisted into a tight knot. Nerves, she told herself. She had not been able to eat breakfast that morning and was not sure that she would manage to eat lunch either.

Félix appeared suddenly at her side.

'This way,' he said without preamble, leading her to a table in the far corner where they would be more private.

A waiter appeared.

'What will you have, Catherine?' Félix asked, holding the menu towards her.

'You order, Félix. But make it something light, if you don't mind.'

Félix placed the order and when the waiter had departed he leaned across the table towards her.

'I was anxious about you,' he said, glancing at her steadily. 'Paul looked so furious when I left that evening, I was certain he was going to strike you.'

Catherine's mouth twisted into the semblance of a smile. 'You need not have been anxious. Paul didn't strike me.'

'Did my presence at your home cause trouble?' he asked then, watching her closely.

Catherine nervously twisted the strap of her handbag. 'Of course not,' she replied, not looking at him. 'Why should it?'

'Come now, Catherine,' Félix said with a slightly cynical twist to his lips. 'You know that I have a ... reputation. Paul knows it too. Did he not think that ... well, that we were ... you know what I mean?'

Catherine felt the colour surge into her cheeks, and Félix was quick to notice it.

'I thought so,' he said bitterly, clenching his fists on the table. 'It is time Paul and I had a long talk. I am not going to let Adèle stop me this time.'

'No, you mustn't do that,' she said quickly. 'Adèle promised me that she would speak to Paul as soon as an opportunity arose. Don't do anything hasty. Not yet ... not until ...'

How could she explain to him the situation at home? She could not tell him of the cold indifference, the explosive silences, Paul was subjecting her to, and of the difficulty of communicating with him. Paul was hardly ever at home and when he condescended to honour her with his presence at home, he would lock himself in his study for the remainder of the evening. Adèle, too, was finding it difficult to approach him, for his mood was black and not at all encouraging for the confession she had to make.

'I will give her this one chance,' Félix agreed, 'but if she does not succeed, I—'

He stopped short, his face paling as his glance swept past Catherine and became riveted to something, or someone, behind her. Fear choked her as she glanced around swiftly. Paul! she thought instantly, but no. Coming towards them at that moment was Eileen Chilton. Catherine had not seen her since the evening they had all dined together at the Château de Bonheur, and she certainly had no wish to meet her at that precise moment.

'Catherine, my dear, it's been simply ages since I last saw you,' Eileen remarked gushingly. 'And you too, Félix. How are you?'

'Quite well, thank you,' Félix replied stiffly, while Catherine murmured something appropriate.

'I never thought I would ever see the two of you lunching together,' Eileen continued slyly. It was obvious that she was bursting with curiosity. 'Do you know each other well?'

The insinuation behind that seemingly innocent question sickened Catherine.

'You forget, Eileen,' Félix replied without hesitation, subjecting her to one of his most charming smiles, 'that Madame de Meillon's husband is a colleague of mine. You forget also that your own husband happens to be a colleague of mine as well. That did not deter you and me from lunching together, did it?' He gave her a meaningful glance. 'And we lunched together often in the past, did we not?'

Eileen became red and flustered, and there was no mistaking the venom in her glance.

'Well, don't let me interrupt your luncheon,' she remarked, recovering her equilibrium, 'and Catherine, do be careful. Félix is rather a naughty boy – or have you discovered that already? 'Bye for now.'

They sat and watched her leave the restaurant with a swinging step, leaving the implication of her remark hovering in the air.

'That woman is a fiend!' Félix expostulated angrily. 'I have always detested a woman who runs after a man, and Eileen Chilton pestered me until I was forced to be rude to her. *Mon dieu!*'

'Do – do you think she'll talk? About seeing us together, I mean?'

'I have no doubt that she will,' Félix hissed through his teeth. 'Eileen Chilton never misses the opportunity to talk and speculate about other people.'

'I knew I shouldn't have come,' Catherine moaned softly.

'It is too late now,' Félix reminded her. 'We can now only hope that by some miracle she will remain silent. Ah, here comes our lunch.'

Catherine was ill when she arrived home that afternoon. She had become increasingly nauseated during the past few weeks and could find no other explanation for it, other than a nervous disorder.

When Susan called at the Château de Bonheur the following day, she found Catherine sitting in the garden looking pale and wan.

'Good heavens! You don't look at all well.'

'I don't feel so well,' Catherine admitted weakly. 'I thought that if I sat in the sun for a moment it would make me feel better. I'm so cold.'

Susan's glance sharpened as she sat down beside

Catherine. 'Have you been to see a doctor yet?'

'It's just a stomach disorder. It will pass.'

'I don't suppose you've considered the possibility that you could be pregnant?'

'Pregnant?' Catherine gasped incredulously. 'No, I couldn't possibly be . . .'

'You are married, you know,' Susan reminded her gently, 'and these things do happen.'

Catherine's thoughts ran wild. It was just impossible, and yet . . .? She had been so concerned lately about the widening chasm between Paul and herself that she had not once stopped to realize what was happening. She glanced at Susan inquiringly.

'Do you think—?'

'I never think, my dear, I leave that part of it to my doctor,' Susan interrupted smilingly. 'Get your coat and let me take you to the doctor quickly.'

It did not take Susan's elderly doctor very long to determine the cause of Catherine's discomfort, and it was with mixed emotions that she eventually stepped out into the sunshine to where Susan waited patiently in the car.

'Well?' Susan prodded gently as Catherine sat staring blankly ahead of her.

'You were right,' she confirmed Susan's suspicions. 'I *am* going to have a child.'

'Oh, my dear, I'm so pleased, and just think how thrilled Paul will be—' Susan ceased her flow of words suddenly as Catherine covered her face with trembling hands. Placing a comforting arm about Catherine's shaking shoulders, she asked: 'What's the matter, Cathy? Have I said something wrong?'

'No.' Catherine dug into her coat pockets to find a handkerchief, and wiped her eyes. 'It's just . . . Oh, Susan, what am I going to do?'

'Do? There's nothing you *can* do, my dear, except allow nature to take its course.'

As they drove home, Catherine wondered whether this news would in any way alter Paul's attitude towards her. Would he be more agreeable to listen to her explanations under the circumstances? Or would he find the idea of becoming a father unpalatable?

'Will you do me a favour, Susan?' she asked as they reached the Château. 'Don't tell anyone just yet. Not even your husband.'

'You don't want Paul to know? You want to surprise him, is that it?'

'Yes,' Catherine agreed, grasping at Susan's explanation, 'I want to surprise him.'

'Very well, Cathy, you can count on my silence.'

For a long time after Susan had left, Catherine remained where she was, loath to enter the house and to face the prying eyes of the servants until she was able to control herself and the tears which threatened to engulf her.

That evening Paul returned home earlier than usual. Catherine heard his slow footsteps coming up the stairs and waited with bated breath until they finally stopped outside her bedroom door. With rapidly beating heart she hastily touched up her lipstick as he knocked lightly before entering.

'You are not well?' he asked, noticing for the first time the shadowy patches beneath her eyes and the hollowness in her cheeks.

'I – I'm quite well, thank you, Paul,' she stammered, avoiding the dark, intense scrutiny of his glance.

'John Dunbury came to see me in my office this afternoon,' Paul said eventually in even tones.

'Oh?' Had Susan, after all, not been able to remain silent? she wondered, instantly alert.

'It is their wedding anniversary on Friday, and we have been invited to have dinner with them at their home.'

'Oh,' she repeated foolishly, relieved that her secret was still safe. 'Did you accept?'

'I told him that I would consult you first.'

An evening out, during which she would have to endure Paul's enforced politeness, was not a very pleasant prospect.

'Do we have to go?' she asked tentatively, clasping and unclasping her hands nervously.

'We cannot really refuse,' he said coldly, and when Catherine nodded acceptance, he added: 'Will you telephone Susan and confirm this?'

After dinner that evening, when Paul had already ensconced himself in his study, Catherine dialled Susan's number.

'Cathy!' Susan exclaimed when she heard who was speaking. 'How are you feeling, my dear?'

'Better, thank you.' She hesitated slightly. 'I believe we've been invited over to have dinner with you on Friday evening?'

'Good heavens, yes,' Susan laughed. 'That's what I actually came over to ask you this morning, but when I found you looking so ill it completely slipped my mind. I really am a terrible scatterbrain. Fortunately I'd asked John to speak to Paul at the Clinic, so I didn't bother you by telephoning.' There was a brief silence. 'Are you coming?'

'Of course,' Catherine replied lightly.

'Good.'

'What time?'

'Will seven o'clock be too early for you?'

'That will suit us perfectly,' Catherine confirmed. 'It will give Paul time to change. I just hope he isn't delayed at the Clinic that evening.'

'I shall be holding thumbs,' Susan said. 'In fact, I shall be holding thumbs for John as well.'

Catherine decided on the pale green silk creation she had bought that afternoon Susan had taken her shopping. Paul had fortunately arrived home early from the Clinic, so there was no need to rush as they would have plenty of time to reach the Dunburys' home on time.

Taking more care than usual with her make-up she set about trying to camouflage the shadows beneath her eyes, as she had no intention of inviting remarks concerning her well-being. There was nothing she could do about her thinness, she decided eventually, and after a last quick inspection of herself in the full-length mirror, she went down to the living-room where she knew Paul would be waiting for her.

'Would you care for a drink before we go?' he asked, hardly glancing at her as she entered. 'There is still time.'

'Yes, please,' she said breathlessly, wondering whether he would at least tell her she looked nice when he condescended to look at her.

She glanced at him surreptitiously while he stood with his back to her, pouring the aperitif. How she loved the way his hair grew into his neck, and the breadth of his shoulders tapering down to his slim hips. But it was his eyes which always had the most devastating effect on her. With one glance he could send her pulse rate soaring or, as of late, chill her to the marrow.

'Your drink,' he said, handing her her glass.

His eyes held hers captive for a moment before sliding deliberately down the length of her, until she quivered expectantly. Now, she thought wildly, he must surely say something now. A solitary drum beat rhythmically in the room as the silence lengthened.

Paul felt the impact of her beauty like a physical blow, but he had succumbed to her appearance once before during their strained relationship, and he had sworn never to do so again.

'Finish your drink,' he instructed coldly, taking a sip of his own.

The drum missed a beat and slowed down. It was only then that Catherine realized she had been listening to her own heartbeat.

When they arrived at the Dunburys' home, there were two other cars parked outside. One belonged to the Chiltons, Catherine discovered to her dismay, and the other to a French couple with a completely unpronounceable surname.

'Call me Mignon,' the dark-haired, sloe-eyed young woman suggested in her heavily accented English. 'My husband is Louis.'

Catherine readily accepted this offer with a grateful smile.

'My dear,' Eileen Chilton spoke suddenly, coming forward to greet them, 'May I say that you do look absolutely devastating? Don't you think so, Paul?'

'Quite,' Paul agreed bluntly.

'Would you like to come and put your coat in my bedroom?' Susan intervened quickly, and Catherine nodded thankfully. She had not bargained with Eileen Chilton being there, and somehow the evening loomed disastrously ahead of her.

'I brought you a small gift,' Catherine said when they were alone, and planting a light kiss on Susan's cheek, she added: 'Happy anniversary.'

'Oh, my dear,' Susan breathed, holding the small, wrapped parcel in her hands. 'You really shouldn't have—'

'Open it,' Catherine interrupted.

Susan fiddled with the string and finally the paper fell away to expose a small replica of a Grecian statue which Susan had admired so much on one of their excursions into the city.

'Oh, Cathy!' she exclaimed excitedly. 'This was most terribly expensive, and wonderfully sweet of you. Oh, how can I thank you enough?'

'Don't thank me. It's I who must thank you for all your kindness and your friendship.'

'Oh, Cathy!' Susan uttered once more, speechless.

'Come,' Catherine said laughingly. 'I've discarded my coat, so let's get back to the others before they start wondering what's happened to their hostess.'

Louis and Mignon, with the unpronounceable surname, lived only two doors away from the Dunbury's, Catherine discovered. They were an extremely amusing couple and kept the conversation flowing at all times. Catherine was grateful for this, for it meant that no one noticed any awkwardness between Paul and herself.

The only person who unnerved her was Eileen Chilton. It did not take Catherine long to realize that Eileen was preening herself for the big moment when she would divulge her information dramatically. Her sly glances and little barbed statements meant nothing to the others, but they filled Catherine with a sense of foreboding as the evening progressed. Tense, and unable to participate in the lighthearted conversation, she waited for Eileen to drop the bombshell which was obviously beginning to burn her fingers.

'More salad, Cathy?' Susan interrupted her train of thought as she made a pretence of eating.

'No, thank you, Susan. Your dinner was absolutely superb.'

'Wait until you've tasted the dessert,' John said mischievously. 'I've never seen such a frivolous concoction in all my life. We've all survived thus far, but I don't guarantee it after you've had the dessert.'

'Men!' Susan managed amid the laughter. 'They just don't appreciate the fact that preparing food is quite an art."

'After tonight I certainly don't deny that fact,' John agreed, shaking with inward laughter, 'but you really excelled yourself when it came to the dessert. It reminds me of this modern rubbish called art. You're not quite sure whether you must eat it, wear it, or take it for a walk.'

There was chaos around the table as everyone shrieked with laughter, and even Catherine felt the icy dread surrounding her heart melt away. Paul, too, appeared more relaxed than she had seen him for some time, Catherine thought as she observed him taking part in this lively debate between Susan and her husband, John.

It was a pleasant evening, in spite of the impending disaster, and there was much laughter once again when Susan triumphantly carried the tray of dessert into the dining-room. It consisted mainly of fruit, beautifully decorated with ice-cream, and not at all as lethal as John had jokingly wanted them to believe.

Later, while having coffee in the living-room, Catherine became nervous and tense once more. She knew herself to be on the brink of disaster – a disaster which she must avoid at all costs, although the problem was, how?

There was a momentary lull in the conversation which terrified her. And then what she had dreaded all evening happened.

'They serve a delightful lunch at a small restaurant

near the Etoile,' Eileen began, glancing at Catherine malevolently.

This was a well-timed remark, as the conversation was still lingering on the subject of exotic dishes and therefore it sounded not at all peculiar. Except to Catherine, who sat rigidly in her chair, knowing that this was exactly what Eileen had been preparing herself for all through dinner.

Ignoring Catherine's pleading glance, Eileen continued unperturbed: 'Catherine can confirm this. I met her there when she was having lunch a few days ago.'

Susan raised a questioning eyebrow when she noticed Catherine's pallor in addition to her look of utter despair. She was about to intervene when Eileen forestalled her. With everyone's attention riveted upon her, she had no intention of allowing Susan to interrupt her little speech.

'I really think you should keep a more watchful eye on your wife, Paul,' she said, turning to face him, satisfied now that she had his complete attention. 'You shouldn't allow Catherine to have lunch with a naughty boy like Félix.'

Catherine's heart beat heavily against her temples, and increased to a deafening crescendo as the room tilted crazily. The only thing she was conscious of was the burning accusation in Paul's eyes.

This was the end, she was certain. She had but one more card to play, and if that failed . . .

During the ensuing silence Louis and Mignon glanced at each other quickly while endeavouring to change the conversation. John coughed, Susan offered more coffee, and Harold Chilton shifted uncomfortably in his chair, sending a distasteful glance in his wife's direction of which she remained sublimely oblivious.

Eileen Chilton had done her job well. She had most probably not intended to be vindictive, and had the situation been different, her statement might have aroused nothing more than a few teasing remarks.

The conversation remained stilted after this and when Paul finally had the opportunity to pass her chair, he whispered disdainfully: 'You are so good at telling lies, make some excuse so that we may leave.'

White to the lips, Catherine asked Susan and John to excuse them as she was not feeling very well. This, in itself, was not a lie, for Catherine felt very ill indeed at that moment.

'What's going on?' Susan whispered anxiously when they were alone for a few seconds in her bedroom while Catherine slipped into her coat.

'I can't explain now,' Catherine whispered back, 'but I really do feel ill.'

'Have you told Paul yet? About the baby, I mean?'

'Not yet.'

'My dear, what are you waiting for?'

What *was* she waiting for? Catherine wondered to herself as they eventually drove home in silence. To wait for a moment of tenderness between them was futile. The silence in the car was deafening, but as neither she not Paul were able to do anything about it, the chilly situation lingered and lengthened. It was only when they entered the house that Catherine decided to play her final card.

Following Paul into his study, she closed the door behind her and faced him tremulously. This situation could not continue for one moment longer, she decided.

'Paul, I would like to explain,' she began tentatively.

'Explain?' he asked harshly, a cynical smile twisting his lips. 'What is there to explain? Unless you expect me to listen to more lies?'

His eyes raked her and the unleashed fury in them sent a shiver of fear through her.

'Félix asked me to meet him because he was anxious about me,' she told Paul truthfully. 'He realized that his presence here must have caused trouble.'

Paul laughed then. It was a harsh sound that set every nerve in her body quivering.

'Félix has never in his life been anxious about the consequences of his escapades,' he said with slow deliberation. 'Try again, Catherine, I may believe your next attempt.'

Catherine was silent for a moment as she faced him. He was completely unrelenting, she realized, and quite immovable where she was concerned.

'I have a very important reason for asking you to allow me to explain.'

'And that is?'

'I'm going to have a baby.' The words came out on a sigh, and had Paul not been so hardened against her, he would have heard the desperate note of pleading in her voice. As it was, he merely experienced the most violent reaction which made him want to lash out and hurt the one person he loved above all else.

'Who is the father?'

Those words struck Catherine like a physical blow and she flinched under their impact as she stood rigidly beside his desk, the colour burning in her cheeks, and then receding to leave her deathly pale.

'In spite of all the damning evidence against me,' she managed through stiff lips, 'you can't seriously believe that I – that Félix—'

She got no further, for the tears brimmed her eyes as

she bit her lip to control its trembling.

'I have no intention of fathering a child which is not mine,' Paul stressed his accusation further with uncaring words.

Catherine's eyes mirrored utter incredulity as she clutched at a chair for support when her whole body began to shake violently.

'I could forgive you almost anything, Paul,' she finally managed through clenched teeth, 'but I shall never forgive you for this!'

Long after Catherine had left the study, Paul stood staring at the door with unseeing eyes. He knew a feeling of shame which made him shift his shoulders uncomfortably in his well cut jacket. He had been driven on by the demon of jealousy and doubt to become the callous brute he was. In spite of all the 'damning evidence', as Catherine had called it, he knew that she was not capable of the things he had accused her of, but he had been unable to control himself, or to break down the wall he himself had built up between them.

He passed a hand over his eyes, as if to wipe from his memory the appalled expression on Catherine's face when he had asked her that hateful question. The look in her eyes was something he would never be able to erase from his memory.

This was something Félix should pay for, he decided as he stormed out of the house and drove at great speed through the gates.

Up in her bedroom, Catherine heard Paul leave. She, too, had had time to make a few decisions of her own. Paul's accusations had been, to her, the final insult, and it had rendered their relationship senseless. Her life had altered drastically over the past few months. From being ideally happy at the start, she had been swept down into the bottomless pit of despair.

Nothing, she was sure, could alter the present situation, and she was not prepared to rear her child in this atmosphere of distrust and chilly politeness.

Hastening down the stairs, she searched in the telephone book for the number she required and eventually lifted the receiver with a shaking hand, and dialled.

'I apologize for telephoning at this late hour,' Catherine said as the receiver was lifted at the other end, 'but I would like to reserve a seat on the next flight to South Africa.'

'*Un moment, madame*,' the man said, and there was a tantalizing silence as she heard him search through his papers. 'You are indeed fortunate, *madame*. There has been a cancellation for the direct flight to Cape Town which leaves at ten-thirty this evening.'

That would give her less than an hour to pack and reach the airport, Catherine realized, but she was determined not to spend another night in this house which held only bitter memories for her.

'Please reserve that seat for me,' she instructed the booking officer at Orly Airport, giving him her name before ringing off and rushing upstairs to pack. There was now only her desperate need to be gone before Paul returned. She could not face him again with the knowledge that he had rejected their child, for with that rejection he had tainted all that had been pure and beautiful between them, leaving only the ashes of memories and a bitterness which was all-engulfing.

CHAPTER TEN

PAUL was in no mood to wait for the lift in the building where Félix had an apartment on the third floor. He raced up the stairs and finally hammered on the door to Félix's apartment instead of pressing the bell. If Félix had not opened the door almost instantly, Paul was ready to break it down. His mood was aggressive, and Félix noticed this as he hastily stood aside for Paul to enter.

'Good evening, *mon ami*,' Félix greeted lightly. He was on the point of turning out the lights before going to bed when Paul had hammered so angrily on his door. 'To what do I owe the pleasure of this unexpected visit?'

'Close the door,' Paul instructed sharply, ignoring Félix's greeting.

Félix did as Paul had ordered and followed him into the living-room of his luxury apartment. He was not at all happy about this visit, for he had a vague suspicion that it concerned his relationship with Adèle, and therefore with Catherine as well.

Paul had no intention of prolonging this visit and immediately came to the point.

'Are you having an affair with my wife?' he asked bluntly, his chest heaving.

'No.'

'Liar!'

Paul's fist shot out with lightning speed, and the next moment Félix lay sprawled on the floor in his silk dressing gown and pyjamas, with an overturned chair beside him. He touched his jaw experimentally where

Paul's fist had landed, but finding everything in order, he smiled ruefully.

'Do you know,' Félix began, not endeavouring to raise himself off the floor, 'it is a long time since an irate husband has knocked me down. But this time it was unnecessary, *mon ami.*'

'Get to your feet and raise your fists,' Paul demanded, towering over the prostrate form of his colleague. 'To-night I shall have the truth even if I have to thrash you to a pulp in the process!'

Félix got to his feet, but his hands remained at his sides. 'Paul, we both know that neither of us can afford to become involved in a brawl. Let us sit down and talk sensibly. If it is the truth you want, then I shall give it to you.'

The calmness with which Félix spoke puzzled Paul, and realizing the logic of Félix's statement, simmered down slightly and allowed Félix to pour them each a stiff cognac.

'You have a very loyal wife,' Félix said, handing Paul his drink. 'Her loyalty even extended as far as Adèle and myself.'

'Adèle? What has Adèle to do with this?'

'Everything.'

Paul was instantly alert. Once before Catherine had tried to involve Adèle in this affair, and now Félix was doing the same. He was not going to have his sister's name dragged through the mud.

'Explain yourself,' he demanded aggressively, and while they drank their cognac, Félix did just that – his childhood, his later life, his love for Adèle, and her fears that Paul would not consider him a suitable husband for her. All this he confessed to Paul. Also how Adèle had made him promise not to approach her brother when he, Félix, had wanted to bring their relationship out into the open, and lastly, of Catherine's part in the whole affair.

'So you see, Paul,' Félix added, 'I have nothing but admiration and respect for your wife, and therefore your suspicions were quite unjustified.'

Paul lapsed into a stunned, self-recriminating silence. What terrible accusations had he not flung at Catherine during these past weeks! He had treated her abominably. It was not more than an hour ago that she had told him she was going to have a child . . . *his* child . . . and he had done the most unforgivable thing by asking her who the father was. What had he done? Why had he allowed his petty doubts to take over and ruin his life . . . indeed, to overrule his common sense?

He looked at Félix, sitting so quietly while awaiting the verdict of the tale he had told. Truly, there had been nothing but honesty and regret on the face of this man whom he had branded an 'amorist and Don Juan'. Are we not all fools at some time or another? Had he himself not been one of the biggest fools just recently?

'Are you rejecting me as a brother-in-law, Paul?' Félix asked eventually, and the hint of anxiety behind those lightly spoken words was clearly evident to Paul.

'I give my permission for the two of you to become engaged, but . . .' he held up his hand to silence Félix as he was about to speak, 'Adèle is still very young, and I demand that you shall not marry for at least a year. During that time you should be able to prove your sincerity, and I shall be satisfied.'

Félix held out a shaking hand. '*Merci*, Paul.'

Paul grasped the hand extended towards him and left soon afterwards. He was in a hurry to get back to

Catherine. He had much to atone for and wanted to waste no time about it.

The Château was in darkness when he arrived, except for the light in the master bedroom. Catherine was still awake, he rejoiced as he raced up the stairs and knocked on her door.

'Catherine?' he called when there was no reply to his knock. For the first time in his life Paul knew real fear as he opened the door and stepped inside quickly.

The bed had not been slept in and the silk evening dress she had worn that evening was on a hanger against the wardrobe. The faint smell of her perfume quivered in his nostrils as he noticed that all her toiletries had been removed from the dressing table. Confirming his suspicions, he pulled open the drawers to find them empty.

He hurried down to his study and searched his desk drawer for Catherine's passport. It was gone! It was clear to him now that Catherine intended leaving him to return to her father in South Africa, and without wasting further time, he left the house and drove to the airport, breaking every speed limit along the way.

Orly Airport was exceptionally busy for that time of night and, causing a few angry glances to be directed at him, Paul practically fought his way to the booking office.

'Have you a Madame de Meillon booked on a flight to South Africa?' he asked the clerk at the counter.

'*Oui, monsieur*,' the clerk confirmed, 'the ten-thirty flight to Cape Town.'

The long hand of the clock on the wall was touching the half hour.

'Which way?' Paul demanded hastily.

The clerk pointed to the exit taken by the passengers. 'But you will be too late, *monsieur*!' he called fruitlessly after Paul's disappearing figure.

Paul had to reach Catherine before the plane took off! He just *had* to stop her! The Boeing was taxiing towards the runway as he reached the gate. He was too late, he realized, pushing an agitated hand through his dishevelled hair. Somewhere inside that gleaming monster was his beloved Catherine, and for the first time he recognized the acute unhappiness which must have driven her to take such a drastic step. It was not going to be an easy task convincing her of his sincerity and regret, but he had every intention of doing just that. Life without Catherine was just unthinkable.

Paul never slept that night. Before leaving the airport, he had booked a seat for himself on the early morning flight to Cape Town. His suitcase was already packed, and although he had changed into pyjamas, sleep evaded him. He paced the floor, smoking numerous cigarettes and deriding himself for his behaviour.

As the first light of dawn appeared in the sky, he sat down and wrote a note to Adèle.

'Catherine left for South Africa last night. By the time you read this I shall be well on my way there as well. My intention is to bring her back, if she will have me after all I have done.

'On my return we will have a serious talk, you and I. For further information contact Félix. Paul.'

On his way out he left the note on the breakfast table where he was sure Adèle would see it. The taxi he had telephoned was already on its way, and he hastily dialled the Clinic, explaining that he would be away for a few days.

It was a tedious flight, for the plane landed at several places on the way. When they finally touched down at Jan Smuts Airport, Johannesburg, he was told that he had an hour to wait for a flight to Cape Town. When he eventually reached his destination early that afternoon, he took the airways bus into town and then drove himself out to Constantia in a hired car.

Sarah, the coloured servant, opened the door to his persistent ringing, and her eyes widened at the sight of Paul standing on the doorstep.

'*Bonjour*,' he greeted her. 'Where is Catherine?'

'Master, I – she is not here,' she stammered as Paul pushed past her.

'Then where is she?' he demanded quietly, turning to face her.

'I don't know, Master Paul.'

Her eyes shifted uncomfortably to the floor and remained there. It was not in her nature to lie, and it was even more difficult to do so when Paul fixed his penetrating glance on her.

'It is important, Sarah, that I speak with her,' Paul continued quietly. 'Tell me where she is.'

Sarah sighed helplessly and shrugged her shoulders. What was the use, she could not lie.

'Miss Cathy arrived home early this morning and left again after taking the key to the master's beach cottage at Gideon's Bay,' she explained. 'She made me promise not to tell Master Charles, or anyone else. Now I've broken my promise,' she ended sadly.

'Do not worry,' Paul said, patting her shoulder, 'I know she will forgive you this time.'

He asked her for directions to Gideon's Bay which she gave him swiftly and clearly.

'Is there trouble, Master Paul?' she asked as he was about to get into the car.

'A misunderstanding,' Paul smiled reassuringly. 'Keep all this to yourself and, Sarah, expect us tomorrow. If all goes well, we shall be staying for a few days.'

Sarah shook her head as she stood and watched him drive off. A misunderstanding? Hmf! She was no fool.

Dressed in an old pair of slacks and a shirt which she found in a cupboard in the spare bedroom, Catherine set about cleaning and airing the cottage. Her tears had long since dried and she was now determined to keep herself occupied until she was able to sit down calmly and sort herself out.

She had taken the train out to Gideon's Bay that morning and had managed to get a lift to the cottage on a pony cart with the old man from the post office who had come to the station to collect the mail. Everything was still very primitive at Gideon's Bay and the local residents were quite happy to keep it that way.

The peace and sanctity of this small place was like balm to her tortured soul. She needed time to think about the future ... a future without Paul.

'I have no intention of fathering a child which is not mine,' Paul had said, and she winced anew at the memory of those words so fiercely spoken. They had cut to the very core of her being and had left her with only one thought in her mind ... to flee from the man who had once held her heart in the palm of his hand.

She had no doubt that when she finally heard the truth from Adèle, he would realize his mistake. But it was already too late, for the damage had been done. Had it been too much to ask for, that Paul should trust her as she had trusted him? Catherine's thoughts were bitter as she stopped her dusting for a moment to stare blindly through the open window.

Later that afternoon she walked along the deserted beach. She was thinking incoherently, and she was tired. She had slept little on the flight out, and even now she was to restless to consider lying down in an effort to rest. She clambered over the rocks until she found a high enough perch from where she could look out to sea and watch the waves rolling in towards the rocky beach. Swimming was dangerous along this part of the coast, but it was a fisherman's paradise. At dawn you found them along these rocks, casting their lines deeper into the sea. Their actions practised, their patience phenomenal, until they were finally rewarded with a fine catch.

Catherine's thoughts were as turbulent as the frothing mass of water that crashed repeatedly against the rocks, sending a fine spray of water into the air to lash her face and arms.

Paul had shown that he had very little faith in her if he could believe her capable of all the things he had accused her of. How would her father react to the news she had to tell him? she wondered. To confront him at this moment was impossible. She needed time to nurse her wounded pride . . . time to grow accustomed to the burning emptiness within her. It would not do to burst into tears when she explained to him her reasons for returning home. To admit that her marriage had been a disaster was not something she was very proud of. She would at least have the child – Paul's child, no matter how much he denied that fact.

'I have no intention of fathering a child which is not mine,' his accusation kept ringing in her ears.

She would not ask him for help if he were the last man on earth! Rearing a child on her own was not going to be easy, she realized, but the baby was hers. Hers! It was all she had left of a beautiful dream.

The tears sprang unbidden to her eyes and fell on cheeks already dampened by the spray. The tide was coming in and the sea's onslaught upon the rocks had become more vicious as the minutes passed. But Catherine was oblivious of everything except her painful thoughts.

A movement on the beach made her turn suddenly. Dressed in a grey light-weight travelling suit, Paul was coming towards her, his arms swaying slightly as he balanced himself while stepping from one rock to the other.

She wondered at the emptiness within her as she watched his approach impassively. It could as well have been a stranger, she thought. When he finally stood towering over her she felt nothing more than a faint curiosity at his presence. What was he going to do? Thrash her? Plead? Or simply carry her off back to France to continue with their senseless marriage for the sake of his reputation; his pride?

No! Her whole being rejected this idea. Nothing on earth would persuade her to return with him!

'You are getting wet,' he rebuked her. 'Do you wish to become ill?'

How typical, she thought with rising hysteria. Always the doctor first, and then the man.

'Would it matter?'

Paul's expression became shuttered. He had not expected a tumultuous welcome, but the chilling reception he was receiving filled him with dread. He had until this moment, been confident of winning her back, but now he was not so sure. It was not going to be easy breaking down the wall of reserve she had built around her during the short space of time which had elapsed since their last, and most damaging, confrontation.

He held out his hand to her, but she ignored it and got to her feet. In silence they stepped over the rocks and walked along the smooth sand to the small cottage on the beach front. The sun had dipped behind the clouds, and the chill in the air made Catherine shiver. She was indeed wet . . . and cold.

Paul's hired car was parked in the driveway, and taking the key from the pocket of her slacks, she unlocked the front door and stepped inside. Paul followed silently in her wake, closing the door against the elements outside.

'Take a hot bath, *chérie*, and change into something warm,' he suggested helpfully.

Catherine whirled on him then. 'Will you kindly stop telling me what to do, and what *not* to do!'

To Paul she had never seemed more beautiful than at that moment, with her green eyes emitting sparks of anger, her legs planted firmly apart, and her hands resting on her shapely hips. Her defiant air aroused him, and it was with the greatest difficulty that he suppressed the desire to seize her in his arms. *Dieu*! how he longed to feel the soft warmth of her in his arms, and the trembling acquiescence of her lips beneath his own.

With a shrug he turned and entered the small lounge. Moments later he heard water being run into the bath, and an involuntary smile curved his lips.

Searching through the teak corner cupboard, he discovered an unopened bottle of wine. Easing the cork off, he poured himself a drink and made himself comfortable. If he knew Catherine, she would make him wait, and the padded armchair with the high back would at least make the wait a pleasant one.

Dieu! he was tired, he thought, closing his eyes for a moment. He had found it impossible to sleep the night before, and during the flight out he had thought of nothing else but Catherine and his own stupidity which had caused her to flee from him with such haste.

He must have dozed, for when he again opened his eyes, the room was in darkness and he could hear someone moving about in the kitchen. Swallowing down the remainder of his drink, he strolled down the passage towards the sound of clattering pots and pans. He found Catherine in front of the gas stove, dressed in a warm woollen dress, with an apron tied about her waist.

'What are you doing?'

'Preparing something for dinner,' she replied without turning. 'I presume you're staying?'

'Am I invited?' he asked, sniffing appreciatively at the odour of steak being grilled.

'I don't appear to have much choice, do I? I must warn you, though, that I don't possess a well stocked larder as I didn't expect to be entertaining guests.'

Paul ventured closer and quite surprisingly, took over the frying of the onions, while she made the omelettes. 'I detect a slight hint of sarcasm in your voice, *chérie*, and it does not suit you.'

She glanced at him then for a brief moment. 'I'm sorry, but you surely didn't expect me to welcome you with open arms?'

Paul removed the frying pan from the stove with a rueful expression on his face. 'Not exactly,' he said, placing the pan to one side and folding his arms as he watched her take the plates from the warming drawer and dish up.

They lapsed into a silence which lasted throughout the uncomfortable meal. Catherine scratched the food about on her plate and finally pushed it aside and sat watching Paul while he devoured the meagre meal she had prepared, as though he had not a care in the world.

'Are you not hungry?' he asked, glancing up to reach

for the salt.

'No.'

Paul shrugged characteristically and continued eating without attempting to make further conversation.

Later, when he suggested helping with the dishes, she declined his offer and sent him through to the lounge, saying that she would bring the coffee through as soon as she was finished.

His presence in the kitchen was disturbing, and she had no wish to prolong the uncomfortable silence between them. On her own she could think, but with Paul hovering about, her thoughts were chaotic and dominated by his presence.

'You didn't exactly waste much time in following me, did you?' she said when she eventually finished the dishes and had served him coffee in the lounge.

'Do you not think that your actions were a little too hasty?' he counter-questioned, his eyes like two dark unfathomable pools.

Catherine considered this a moment and when she spoke, she found it difficult to control the quivering of her voice. 'Do you ... in the circumstances ... consider my actions were hasty?' She swallowed painfully. 'Would you, if you had been in my position, not have done the same?'

He shrugged. 'I am a man. Men react differently to certain situations.'

'Of course!' Her voice sounded thin and brittle. 'You *would* react differently. You are cool to the point of cruelness, entirely without emotion, and incapable of ever behaving irrationally.'

Paul was white about the mouth. 'Those are harsh words, *chérie*, and you know they are not true.'

'Do I? Do I, Paul?' she asked, biting her lip to stop

its trembling. 'I don't know what to think any more.'

'Catherine, there is something I must explain.'

'There is nothing to explain, Paul,' she interrupted him, getting to her feet and walking about the room as though to find some relief for pain which had lodged itself in the region of her heart.

'From the time we returned to Paris, after our honeymoon in the South of France, you changed,' she continued, ceasing her relentless pacing now to face him as all the bitterness overflowed into words. 'You became cool and aloof, snatching at each and every excuse to drive the wedge in further between us. It started the night we gave that dinner party. Shortly afterwards you moved out of our bedroom into the dressing-room, and I became no more to you than a servant in your home.'

'That is not true!'

'Oh, yes,' she laughed cynically. 'I was forgetting the night you entered my bedroom to inform me of your early departure the following morning, when you had to attend that conference in London. You were at least human then!' Again she laughed bitterly. 'I thought then that somehow you still needed me and that in spite of everything, you did still love me. I believed, foolishly, that matters would improve. But the next morning I found your cryptic little note, and realized that you'd merely needed a woman. Any woman! And I had been available. Oh, God, how available I'd been!'

The tears came then, chasing each other down her cheeks as anguished sobs shook her slender frame. Paul felt as though he had been rooted to his chair as he watched her. He realized for the first time how deeply he had hurt her by his callous behaviour, and cursed himself, for the thousandth time, that he could have been such an utter fool.

'I tried to understand the reason for your actions,' she continued presently when she was able to control herself once more. 'I forgave you because you were unaware of the truth, and because I knew of your fear that I'd married you out of gratitude. But I can't forgive you for thinking that I'm going to have another man's child.'

Paul was on his feet then. His one aim was to comfort her, and beg her forgiveness.

'Don't touch me!' she cried, backing away from him as she anticipated his move.

Resigning himself to her will, he dropped his hands to his sides. He would have to tread carefully, he realized, for their future together depended on it.

'When I left you last night, I went straight to Félix,' he told her, and was rewarded by a flicker of interest in her level glance. 'It was not a pleasant meeting, but I am now in possession of the true facts.'

'Is that why you followed me at such speed?'

Her words stung, yet he knew that he deserved them to some extent. 'I would have come even without that knowledge.'

'Would you have, Paul? I wonder!'

Once again there was that cynical twist to her lips which was so uncommon to her nature. Her glance was thoughtful as it rested upon him. Could she believe him, or was it merely the disgrace of a broken marriage that made him utter that statement? So many questions crowded her mind, and woven through them were a thousand new doubts which had suddenly been born.

'Why did you not come to me in the first place?' Paul interrupted her thoughts. 'If you had done so, then none of this would have happened.'

'It would have happened, no matter what the circumstances, Paul. It was like a festering wound that had to be cleansed. Besides, I promised Adèle that I would remain silent.'

'Why?'

'She was afraid of what you might do,' Catherine explained agitatedly. 'But you know all this, for Félix must have told you.'

The clock on the mantelshelf ticked loudly as a brooding silence settled in the room. It was then that Catherine noticed the tired droop of Paul's shoulders, the greyness of his complexion and the lines of suffering on either side of his mouth. For a moment her heart softened towards him, and then she steeled herself once more. Had he not made her suffer too?

'Am I so entirely without understanding that neither you nor Adèle could approach me with that problem?' Paul asked slowly, lighting a cigarette and lowering himself once more into the comfort of the armchair. For a moment he watched the smoke curl lazily up towards the ceiling before glancing at her inquiringly. 'Am I, *chérie*?'

Now it was Catherine's turn to feel the sting of his rebuke, as walking across to the window, she stared out into the inky blackness beyond.

'No, Paul, I can't say you're without understanding,' she replied sincerely, her back towards him. 'Once, when I needed it most, you gave your understanding without hesitation. I haven't forgotten.'

A restful silence followed this remark. It was as though the tenseness had disintegrated between them, leaving them both calm and able to think clearly.

'Why did you follow me?' she asked eventually, keeping her face averted.

She heard him crush his cigarette into the ashtray, and the next moment he was standing behind her. So close, in fact, that she could smell his particular brand of shaving cream, and the faint odour of tobacco which always clung to him. Her treacherous heart beat wildly against her ribs.

'I came to take you back with me,' he said simply, his breath fanning her neck and filling her with a wild desire to escape before it was too late.

'It's as simple as that, is it?' she asked tersely. 'You followed me all the way out here, with only one thought in mind, and that was to take me back to France with you? Well, I'm sorry you had to make such a fruitless journey, because I have no intention of going back with you.'

Paul's hands came down heavily on to her shoulders as he turned her roughly to face him.

'I think, perhaps, I have not made myself clear. I am asking ... no, begging you to come back with me.' There was sincere penitence in his steady glance, and a touch of desperation in the agonizing pressure of his fingers on her shoulders. '*Dieu*, Catherine,' he groaned, 'I cannot forgive myself for the hurt I have caused you, and I despise myself for what I said last night about ... about the child. I regretted it the moment you left my study, but I was too angry at the time ... yes, and too proud to follow you and apologize. *Mon coeur*, will you not forgive me?'

He drew her, for a moment unresisting, into his arms. Then she broke free, her expression resembling that of a frightened little animal as the soft glow of the gas lamp lit her face.

'No! How do I know that you won't start doubting me again at some future date?' she cried, wringing her hands in despair. 'I can't go through another time like the one I've just been through.'

'*Chérie*, you have my word—'

'No, Paul,' she interrupted quickly, her voice slightly unsteady. 'I appreciate the fact that you're sorry, and I accept your apologies, but . . . you'll always have that niggling doubt at the back of your mind that I just might have married you out of gratitude, and nothing more. And then, at the least little thing, you'll become suspicious, and we'll find ourselves back where we were just recently.'

They faced each other in silence, and Paul knew a feeling of helplessness as he realized the implication of her words. There was no way he could prove to her that his old doubts no longer existed, and if she would not give him the opportunity by returning to him, then his plight was hopeless.

'*Chérie*, there is a slender thread linking love and gratitude, and the latter can so easily be mistaken for the other. For love. You were my patient, and for you I performed a miracle, with the help of *le bon dieu*. You could so easily have been influenced by the success of that operation. You cannot entirely blame me for doubting you, and knowing Félix for what he was only served to increase that doubt.' Paul was finding it difficult to continue as the muscles in his throat tightened. 'I realize now that I need never have doubted you, for it was all of my own making, and born of my own fears.' He hesitated, his dark eyes lit by a sudden gleam. 'I want only your happiness, *chérie*. If you wish me to go, then I will do so. But the decision rests with you.'

His words were like a searing pain through her heart. He was prepared to return to France without her if she had no wish to continue their marriage. The long years of loneliness spread like a chasm before her, years during which she would have only their child to lavish her love and care on. Suddenly her whole being came into revolt against the picture that flashed before her eyes. Her throat tightened, emotion robbing her of speech and, taking her silence to signify rejection, Paul turned slowly and walked towards the door, utterly beaten.

'Paul!'

Her voice was the merest whisper, but in the silence of the autumn night, with only the sound of the waves breaking on the shore, Paul heard her. Turning quickly, he was just in time to catch her in his arms.

They clung together as though they could not bear the thought of letting each other go. Caressing lips and straining arms said more than words ever could. They kissed, long and satisfyingly, and when the storm of passion had finally spent itself, he pulled her down on to the couch beside him, and held her in his arms with her head resting on his shoulder.

'*Mignonne*, I love you most desperately,' Paul said, his voice thick with emotion. 'I swear, before *le bon dieu*, that I shall make it up to you for all the unhappiness you have suffered.'

'Oh, Paul, Paul, darling,' she managed through her tears. 'I love you with every part of my being, and you need never, ever doubt that again.'

'Forgive me, *chérie*,' he said, but she silenced him with a gentle finger against his lips.

'No more apologies, my darling,' she whispered, 'after all, I too was at fault. I should have let you into the secret right at the beginning. Oh,' she sat upright suddenly, 'I almost forgot. What have you decided about Adèle and Félix?'

Paul explained briefly what had transpired between himself and Félix.

'I did not trust myself to speak to Adèle before I left,' he concluded, his lips tightening. 'She will certainly have a lot to answer for.'

'No,' Catherine shook her head seriously. 'Let it all be forgotten now. We're together again, and that's all that matters.'

'You are most generous, *mon coeur,* and I hope Adèle appreciates that fact,' he smiled, taking her back into his arms.

It was much later when Catherine told her adoring husband that she would have to prepare the main bedroom for them.

'But why?' Paul asked innocently.

'I didn't expect you to turn up here and prepared only a single bed in the spare room for myself,' she explained, going crimson at the expression in his eyes.

'For one night I shall not mind sharing a single bed with you,' Paul suggested, crushing her to his breast. 'In the morning we shall return to Cape Town and tell your father that he is to become a grandfather in the not too distant future. Perhaps we shall remain a few days before returning to France.'

'Oh, Paul, that would be heaven,' she sighed ecstatically against his lips.

'Heaven is here, *mon coeur,*' he replied before claiming her lips, and Catherine knew this to be the truth. Heaven was indeed here in Paul's arms.

romance is beautiful!

**and Harlequin Reader Service
is your passport to the
Heart of Harlequin**

Harlequin is the world's leading publisher of romantic fiction novels. If you enjoy the mystery and adventure of romance, then you will want to keep up to date on all of our new monthly releases—eight brand new Romances and four Harlequin Presents.

If you are interested in catching up on exciting and valuable back issues, Harlequin Reader Service offers a wide choice of best-selling novels reissued for your reading enjoyment.

If you want a truly jumbo read and a money-saving value, the Harlequin Omnibus offers three intriguing novels under one cover by one of your favorite authors.

To find out more about Harlequin, the following information will be your passport to the Heart of Harlequin.

collection
editions

**Rare Vintage Romance
From Harlequin**

The Harlequin Collection editions have been chosen from our 400 through 899 series, and comprise some of our earliest and most sought-after titles. Most of the novels in this series have not been available since the original publication and are available now in beautifully redesigned covers.

When complete, these unique books will comprise the finest collection of vintage romance novels available. You will treasure reading and owning this delightful library of beautiful love stories for many years to come.

For further information, turn to the back of this book and return the INFORMATION PLEASE coupon.

the omnibus

A Great Idea! Three great romances by the same author, in one deluxe paperback volume.

A Great Value! Almost 600 pages of pure entertainment for only $1.95 per volume.

Essie Summers

Bride in Flight (#933)
...begins on the eve of Kirsty's wedding with the strange phone call that changed her life. Blindly, instinctively Kirsty ran — but even New Zealand wasn't far enough to avoid the complications that followed!

Postscript to Yesterday (#1119)
...Nicola was dirty, exasperated and a little bit frightened. She was in no shape after her amateur mechanics on the car to meet any man, let alone Forbes Westerfield. He was the man who had told her not to come.

Meet on My Ground (#1326)
...is the story of two people in love, separated by pride. Alastair Campbell had money and position — Sarah Macdonald was a girl with pride. But pride was no comfort to her at all after she'd let Alastair go!

Jean S. MacLeod

The Wolf of Heimra (#990)
...Fenella knew that in spite of her love for the Island, she had no claim on Heimra yet — until an heir was born. These MacKails were so sure of themselves; they expected everything to come their way.

Summer Island (#1314)
...Cathie's return to Loch Arden was traumatic. She knew she was clinging to the past, refusing to let it go. But change was something you thought of happening in other places — never in your own beloved glen.

Slave of the Wind (#1339)
...Lesley's pleasure on homecoming and meeting the handsome stranger quickly changed to dismay when she discovered that he was Maxwell Croy — the man whose family once owned her home. And Maxwell was determined to get it back again.

Susan Barrie

Marry a Stranger (#1034)
...if she lived to be a hundred, Stacey knew she'd never be more
violently in love than she was at this moment. But Edouard had told her
bluntly that he would never fall in love with her!

Rose in the Bud (#1168)
...One thing Cathleen learned in Venice: it was highly important to be
cautious when a man was a stranger and inhabited a world unfamiliar to
her. The more charm he possessed, the more wary she should be!

The Marriage Wheel (#1311)
...Admittedly the job was unusual — lady chauffeur to Humphrey
Lestrode; and admittedly Humphrey was high-handed and arrogant.
Nevertheless Frederica was enjoying her work at Farthing Hall. Then
along came her mother and beautiful sister, Rosaleen, to upset
everything.

Violet Winspear

Beloved Tyrant (#1032)
...Monterey was a beautiful place to recuperate. Lyn's job was
interesting. Everything, in fact, would have been perfect, Lyn Gilmore
thought, if it hadn't been for the hateful Rick Corderas. He made her feel
alive again!

Court of the Veils (#1267)
...In the lush plantation on the edge of the Sahara, Roslyn Brant tried
very hard to remember her fiancé and her past. But the bitter,
disillusioned Duane Hunter refused to believe that she ever was
engaged to his cousin, Armand.

Palace of the Peacocks (#1318)
...Suddenly the island, this exotic place that so recently had given her
sanctuary, seemed an unlucky place rather than a magical one. She
must get away from the cold palace and its ghost — and especially from
Ryk van Helden.

Isobel Chace

The Saffron Sky (#1250)
...set in a tiny village skirting the exotic Bangkok, Siam, the small,
nervous Myfanwy Jones realizes her most cherished dream, adventure
and romance in a far-off land. Two handsome men determine to marry
her, but both have the same mysterious reason....

A Handful of Silver (#1306)
...in exciting Rio de Janeiro, city of endless beaches and skyscraper
hotels, a battle of wits is waged between Madelaine Delahaye, Pilar
Fernandez, the jealous fiancée of her childhood friend, and her
handsome, treacherous cousin — Luis da Maestro....

The Damask Rose (#1334)
...Vicki Tremaine flies to the heady atmosphere of Damascus to meet
Adam Templeton, fiancé of the rebellious Miriam. But alas, as time
passes, Vicki only becomes more attracted to this young Englishman
with the steel-like personality....

Jane Arbor

A Girl Named Smith (#1000)
...Mary Smith, a girl with a most uninspired name, a mouselike personality and a decidedly unglamorous appearance. That was how Mary saw herself. If this description had fitted, it would have been a great pleasure to the scheming Leonie Crispin and could have avoided a great deal of misunderstanding between Mary, Leonie and the handsomely attractive Clive Derwent....

Kingfisher Tide (#950)
...Rose Drake was about to realize her most cherished dream — to return to the small village of Maurinaire, France. The idea of managing her aunt's boutique shop produced grand illusions for Rose, but from the very day of her arrival, they were turned to dismay. The man responsible was the town's chief landowner and seigneur, a tyrant — living back in the days of feudalism....

The Cypress Garden (#1336)
...at the Villa Fontana in the Albano Hills in Italy, the young, pretty Alessandra Rhode is subjected to a cruel deception that creates enormous complications in her life. The two handsome brothers who participate pay dearly for their deceit — particularly, the one who falls in love....

Anne Weale

The Sea Waif (#1123)
...it couldn't be, could it? Sara Winchester, the beautiful and talented singer, stood motionless gazing at the painting in the gallery window. As she tried to focus through her tears, her thoughts went racing back to her sixteenth birthday, almost six years ago, and the first time she had set eyes on the sleek black-hulled sloop *Sea Wolf* and its owner, Jonathon "Joe" Logan....

The Feast of Sara (#1007)
...as Joceline read and re-read the almost desperate letter just received from cousin Camilla in France, pleading with Joceline to come and be with her, she sensed that something was terribly wrong. Immediately, she prepared to leave for France, filled with misgivings; afraid of learning the reason for her cousin's frantic plea....

Doctor in Malaya (#914)
...Andrea Fleming desperately wanted to accompany the film crew on the expedition, but Doctor James Ferguson was adamantly opposed, stating that if she went along, he would refuse to guide them. But Guy Ramsey had other ideas, and cunningly devised a scheme whereby Andrea would join them — in a manner the Doctor could do nothing about....

information please

**All the Exciting News from
Under the Harlequin Sun**

It costs you nothing to receive our news bulletins and
intriguing brochures. From our brand new releases to our
money-saving 3-in-1 omnibus and valuable best-selling
back titles, our information package is sure to be a hit.
Don't miss out on any of the exciting details. Send for
your Harlequin INFORMATION PLEASE package today.